Curious

LESLIE MCADAM

About this book

I'm desperately attracted to my husband. Which wouldn't be a problem, except he's straight.

What happened is, my longtime crush/hero got badly injured saving me from my evil ex-boyfriend. When I found out he (my hero, not my ex) didn't have health insurance, I did the logical thing: I proposed. To my surprise, he said yes.

I knew that Camden wasn't interested in me *like that*. This deal was always meant to be temporary—just until he healed and could get his own insurance and I found a place to stay, since I'm not moving back in with my ex. No feelings involved.

Except Cam kissed me at our wedding ceremony, and ever since, we can't seem to stop kissing. He says he's curious what sex with a man would be like, but I don't want to be another straight guy's experiment.

Still, Cam is so kind and beautiful, with his dark eyes and tousled curls shoved into a backward baseball cap. His patience makes me want to throw out all my carefully crafted rules. And don't get me started on how his first instinct is to protect me ...

But I'm scared if I open my heart, I'm going to get hurt. Again.

Can I risk telling Cam how I feel before our deal ends? Or should I let him go and lose the best (fake) relationship I've ever had?

Curious is a stand-alone contemporary M/M romance novel with a marriage of convenience and bisexual awakening. It features Shelby, a receptionist who's never met a vision board he didn't like; Camden, an internet-famous contractor; and a hasty wedding for medical insurance reasons. Happy ever after guaranteed.

Author's note

Did I intend the insurance scenario described in this book to portray reality? No.

Did I do my research on it? Also no.

Could someone get an appointment for a next-day wedding at any of the seven county clerks' offices in Los Angeles? Almost assuredly no. (Although I hear there are third parties who will obtain a same-day license and do the ceremony for you.)

For that matter, can you get on-street parking in Los Angeles in front of a store without paying for it? Or make it from Century City to the Valley and back on a lunch break? Or hang out with the biggest rock star on the planet? I mean, it's possible, but infinitely more probable between the pages of a book. (And a certainty in this one.)

In short, this book requires suspension of disbelief on the part of the reader in the name of fiction, fun, romance, and love. That said ...

Content warning: Domestic violence, violence (on page), neglectful/emotionally abusive childhood history.

CHAPTER 1

Camden

The afternoon sun beats on my nape and sweat trickles down my scalp as I kneel on a composition shingle roof, using my nail gun. Late summer in Los Angeles means hot, windy days with the scent of eucalyptus wafting in the air. I yank off my backward baseball cap, run my fingers through my damp hair, and wipe my forehead on my flannel-covered bicep.

And, ahem, if you're an OSHA inspector, no, I don't need a hard hat up here, as there's no possible danger of head injury from falling or flying objects. I've got no chance of getting hurt today.

I take a moment to look around, because I always like the perspective from a rooftop. It's rare that anyone experiences this exact perspective, and I dunno. I just dig it, though the view's not that exciting today: trees, adjacent houses, distant high-rises, and the ever-present traffic on the 101. A newer silver Civic recently pulled into the driveway next door, but otherwise it's been pretty quiet on this street. Very few distractions to keep me from doing the job, which I'm almost finished with.

So I'm about ready for a shower and a beer. In that order. I put my cap back on and survey my handiwork. It looks good. I'm pleased.

We're reroofing a small 1960s tract house on a cul-de-sac in the San Fernando Valley. I attach the final shingles of my section, then yell to David, my roofing subcontractor, who's working at the other end of the roof, "You 'bout done over there?"

"Yeah, almost." His nailer keeps up its repetitive thunk. "Okay," he calls back a moment later. "Last ones."

"I'll start mopping up." My phone buzzes with a text, but when I pull it out to see who it's from, I get a sinking feeling in my gut.

Nope. Not talking to her. Not today or ever again. I don't wanna hear it.

Grumbling, I adjust my tool belt, hoist up a leftover bundle of shingles, and back my way down the ladder to the ground. Once there, I take off the tool belt and kneepads. I stash all the equipment away in the back of the truck, then scan for anything we've left behind. A moment later, David joins me on the ground, carrying his own bundle. I sling the ladder over my shoulder and secure it to the rooftop rack.

We're done with this project and will move on to the next tomorrow, on schedule. David waves, climbs into his own truck, and takes off. I do a log entry so I can invoice the homeowner, then go to get in the driver's seat ... but I pause with my boot in the footwell, because I hear yelling from next door.

Male voices. Loud yelling.

Like, *this is not a joke* loud.

I freeze, rooted to the spot—abs and thighs clenching, hand gripping the door so tight my knuckles are white, my body readying for fight or flight. I never know in situations with strangers whether I should get involved, and if so, how.

But I gotta do something, I think. It sounds *bad*.

Before I can move, it's suddenly very quiet. Then a door slams, and a person small enough to be a young teenager races out of the neighbor's house. My adrenaline spikes, because I recognize the man: Shelby Borchard, the competent, cheerful receptionist at the law firm where my brother and sister work. I'm straight, but thanks to my siblings, I know the lingo. He's a twink.

I've been to a few firm gatherings, and while Weston & Ramirez has plenty of employees, Shelby sticks out, mostly because of his looks—he's got platinum blond hair that's in sharp contrast to his dark umber eyes and tawny skin—but also because of his friendly and outgoing personality.

But he sticks out even more right now, since his normally immaculate appearance is disheveled: barefoot, hair mussed, and tight, bright pink polo shirt ripped. That makes some inner beast inside me roar.

Shelby's wearing a backpack, has a few duffel bags slung over his shoulders, and is carrying a cardboard box. He stubs his toe on the concrete and curses quietly. He tosses the bags and box in the trunk of the Civic I noticed earlier and books it toward the driver's side door.

Before I know what I'm doing, I sprint down the sidewalk and over the grass to him. He sees me as he's reaching a shaking hand toward the car door and startles. "Cam-Camden? What? Why?"

Shelby has a bruise blooming on his cheek, and he's wild-eyed, his face stained with tears.

Anger flares inside me, and my hands ball into fists. Not to hurt him, obviously. "What happened? Who did this?" I demand, noticing his split lip and what could be the beginning of a black eye.

"It's fine," he says, his lip trembling and his eyes looking anywhere but at me.

"Bullshit." My voice comes out in a deep growl. "Who hurt you?"

"It's nothing." He steps gingerly toward the car, since he's not wearing shoes. At least, I hope that's why he's moving that way. If he's been hit anywhere else ...

He opens the door, but I put my arm out, blocking him from getting in. I don't want to scare him, but I also don't want whoever did this to him to get away with it. "It doesn't look like nothing. Let me see." He sighs and finally looks up at me. I inspect his face, cradling his jaw with my palms, and I turn ragey. Again, not at him. "I'm not going to ask again," I say very quietly. "Who did this to you?"

"No one." He sucks in his lip, winces in pain, and pulls back from me, and I let him move past me to sit in the car. His whole body is trembling now.

I give him a hard look.

He squeezes his eyes shut, then relents. "My boyfriend."

That makes me blink. "Your *boyfriend* did this to you? What the hell kind of—"

"My *ex*-boyfriend," he mutters. I don't miss his flinch from processing that he went from a boyfriend to an ex in the space of, what? This afternoon? A few minutes? He looks scared and angry and roughed up.

I'm looming over him, but it's because I want to put a wall around him so no one will ever do anything like this again. I can be a protective barrier against the world and whatever he's vulnerable to. "Shelby. What. Happened?"

"He's pissed because I found out about him," he mumbles. He gazes at me, resigned. "I just moved in with him—haven't even unpacked all the way—and I got home from work early. I walked in all chipper and calling to him, but he was talking to someone on the phone." Shelby's lip juts out, and tears well in his eyes. "His goddamn *wife*, who lives in New York." He swallows. "He's a talent agent, and I thought his trips out of town were to check on shows there. So apparently yeah, he did do that, but he also was living with his *family* back east. His wife heard my voice, and she started yelling, so loud even I could hear it, and then he hung up the phone and turned on me."

"He put his hands on you?" My voice is very low.

Shelby looks away.

My blood's boiling. I don't consider myself to be particularly violent, but I get pissed at bullies, especially those who pick on people smaller than they are. I had plenty of experience in school defending Charlie and Reyna, my two younger siblings, both of whom are queer. I'm bigger and have always been in charge of keeping them safe.

I'm feeling protective about Shelby right now. Most of the time I'm easygoing, but things like this set me off. While, from what I've seen at Weston & Ramirez parties, Shelby has the mouth to be able to tell anyone off, he's so little there's no way he could win a fight. Even a fair fight. And I'd wager whoever roughed him up didn't play fair by any means.

Even though some part of me knows this situation is none of my business, I can't let it go. Shelby's become my business because he's part of my siblings' professional lives.

I stalk up to the house, boots clomping loudly on the walk, and knock on the door.

"Camden!" Shelby calls, following me, his bare feet silent. "*Don't.*"

"Don't what?" I ask, facing him. I'm trying to be gentle with him, even though my heart is thundering in my ears and my hands keep clenching into fists.

"Just ... just forget it. Please." He gives me these big, pleading eyes, and for a moment, I'm tempted to turn back. "He'll calm down. I'll get my stuff later."

"He shouldn't get away with treating you like that."

The door opens, and a male voice behind me says, "Who shouldn't get away with what?"

The man in the doorway is fit, maybe in his thirties, with light brown hair and a slick look to him, but he's quivering with suppressed rage.

"Evan," Shelby whispers. "We were just, um. Going—"

I step closer and ask in a quiet voice, "Did you hit Shelby?"

Evan scoffs and cracks his knuckles. "My renter? He tripped. Kind of clumsy."

"Bullshit," I snarl. "Your *renter*? He's your dirty little secret, isn't he? Your wife didn't know you're in the closet. God, you're a pathetic loser."

"I think you need to leave." Evan takes a step outside and gets in my face. I'm taller, but he's a little bigger. Not much. I'm in better shape, I think, from all the physical work I do. This guy looks like he goes to the gym, but that doesn't mean he actually knows how to fight.

I was in plenty of fights as a teenager, but since I left my twenties, I thought I'd left that crap behind me.

Except I can't let this asshole get away with hurting people. "I think you need to be better," I tell him. "Don't ever fucking lay a hand on anyone else, let alone someone smaller than you. You think you're such a big man, but you're just scared. It's obvious."

"Cam," Shelby says, tugging on the sleeve of my flannel. "Drop it."

There's a lot more I'd like to say to this loser—preferably with my fists—but Shelby deserves to have someone pay attention to what he wants. I needed to size up the asshole who had the absolute gall to fuck with Shelby. Now that I know what I'm dealing with, I'll do what Shelby says. I nod and address Evan. "We'll come back to get Shelby's things. We'll give you a heads-up so you can be somewhere far away."

"Far, far away," Shelby mutters. "Ugh. He's not worth it. I can't believe I wasted my time with him. I can't believe he has a *wife*. Bastard."

I take a deep breath and turn to walk away, but out of the corner of my eye, I catch a glimpse of Evan making a fist. He lunges for Shelby, muttering, "You fucked my life up, you little shit."

My reflexes are fast, and I step in between them and punch Evan hard in the nose. He yelps and aims for me instead. I sidestep him easily and hit him again in the face, ignoring the way my knuckles sting. Then a fist in the gut. He's doubled over and swearing, and while some part of me wants to keep whaling on him, I can maintain control. "Pick on someone your own size, jackass," I grit out.

Blood is starting to trickle out of his nose, and he spits on me. "I'll sue you for assault."

"Do it," I sneer. "I'm related to two lawyers."

Even bent over, he attempts to make a fist and pull his arm back, but Shelby yells, "Stop it. Both of you."

I glance over at him and, okay, *enough*. I hold up my hands and address Evan. "Fine. Except. You pick on him, you answer to me."

"Whatever," Evan says, spitting blood. "Take that piece of trash with you, asshole, and don't come back."

I shake my head, wanting to keep defending Shelby, but I made my point. I'll let Evan get the last word. That's fine. I have nothing to prove, and Shelby seems safe.

Except just then, Evan shoves me hard on his way to, I don't know, punch Shelby one last time. I push back, throwing my body between the two of them, but I step wrong on my ankle, bending it at a weird angle off the cement and into the landscaping. Something cracks. I catch myself before I fall, but not before I fuck up my leg. *Bad*.

"Oh, fuck," I groan. I stand up and attempt to put weight on my ankle, but it crumples. So I balance on the one that's still good.

Then I coldcock the guy, and he falls to the ground.

Shelby's trembling. His face is gray. "I can't believe you knocked him out."

"I'm so sorry you had to see that," I pant, shaking out my fist, blood pumping in my ears. "I'm sorry he treated you that way."

"He deserved it." He looks down and points at my ankle. "What should we do about that?"

"I'm sure it's just sprained," I say, even though searing fire is running through it. "No big deal. I'll wrap it and ice it and take some Tylenol."

"Let me take you to an urgent care."

I shake my head. "No, that won't work. I don't have health insurance." Not anymore. I lost everything because of her.

"What?"

"I'm a general contractor. I'm on my own. I have to carry workers' comp, but this isn't that. So I'll go home, and I'll deal. Don't worry."

"I will worry. What if it's worse than a sprain?"

"It's fine." In fact, it hurts more than I'm willing to admit, and I'm wondering if this is one of those adult-type injuries like sleeping wrong or sneezing, where a little thing becomes a big-deal pain in the rear. Except, unlike those passive injuries, I was pushed.

But still—back in the day, I'd skateboard, ride bikes, snowboard and ski, jump off a roof into a pool and not think twice about it. If I got hurt, most of the time I bounced back fast.

Getting older sucks, although I'm not old. Thirty-one isn't old.

Evan moans, and I look at Shelby. "Where are you planning on going right now?"

He comes up under my arm and helps support me. He's sturdier than he looks, and he smells minty. "I think you need to get that looked at."

"It's fine," I repeat. "Where are *you* going?"

He sighs. "I have no idea. I figured I'd get in my car and then find a coffee shop and look online for an Airbnb or a hotel."

"Where did you move from? Can you go back?"

"No. I gave my notice at my last place, and the landlord had someone lined up right away. It's okay. I can afford a hotel for a while."

With his help, I kind of shuffle-limp to my truck. I pause before getting in. "Come home with me," I blurt. "I live pretty close, and I've got a pool house you can stay in tonight. Or for a couple nights."

He shakes his head. "No, it's okay. I'll go find a hotel."

"Don't," I say. "Please. Come home with me. Let's get you

some ice for that lip." I give him a sheepish grin. "My house is a construction zone, but the pool house is all fixed up. I just finished it."

Shelby looks forlornly at Evan's house and at his car. "Um. I'm not sure. Wouldn't your ... I mean, do you live with anyone?"

I shake my head. How much have my siblings told him about me? "No, I live alone. No wife or girlfriend. I'm single. No roommate. No one."

"Okay. Um. I guess I could come over for tonight, at least. That way I can help you with that ankle."

"Deal. We'll break out the first aid kit for you, too. Give me your phone."

He furrows his brows.

"You can follow me there, but in case you get lost or we get separated."

Shelby fishes the phone out of his bag and hands it to me, open. I create a new contact, *Camden Cooper*, and then text myself.

I give him back his phone. "You're all set. Follow me."

CHAPTER 2

Shelby

I'm pretty sure today is the second-worst day of my life—my eighteenth birthday gets top honors—except it's kind of the best, too.

As I follow Cam's truck, the rubber accelerator feeling foreign under my bare foot, I slowly start being able to breathe easier. I ran from Evan, but not before he got a few hits in, mostly in areas covered by my clothes. I'm going to be bruised tomorrow, and I keep shaking.

Evan seemed like a different person just now. I've never been more scared in my life—the way he lashed out at me when he realized his wife had found out he's a cheater. And, apparently, when she found out he wasn't straight.

He should've thought of potential fallout before he started anything up with me, and yet somehow, it's my fault? I'm so pissed. I've gone from being scared shitless to feeling numb. The tears have dried, and I'm just trying to unpack the past twenty minutes or so. I don't know where to start.

Actually, I do: with Cam Cooper.

When he appeared like some kind of avenging angel in denim and flannel, I had no idea who he was for a moment. Here's some random guy running at me, and I was a bit terrified life was going to get worse. Was he going to attack me, too? It's not like my mind was working rationally after Evan turned on me.

But then I focused, and I couldn't believe it was *him*. Cam's so gorgeous, I never know where to look first. Deep, dark sepia-colored eyes, skin that's tan from working outside, well-groomed scruff on his cheeks and jaw. He's one of those big but rangy guys who's strong, agile, and gets shit done.

So, of course, I've had a crush on him in the worst way since I first laid eyes on him. It's not just me, though. He's internet famous. His brother, Charlie, an attorney in my office, films their DIY projects together. I've maybe watched one or two—cough, *dozen*, cough—of their time-lapse videos on Ad/VICE, a newer social media platform. I pretty much only use it to watch Cam's videos, because OMG have you seen the man? He's unbelievable.

Cam is blue-collar through and through, and I love the messy curls of his dark brown hair, which is normally stuffed into a backward baseball cap, like now. He's always in jeans and a flannel over a T-shirt, at least the times I've seen him at firm events and in his videos.

This crush goes one way, though, like all my crushes do. From what I know based on the chatter in the office, I think Cam's only dated women. In fact, there was talk of a wedding a year ago or so? Maybe? Well, he's likely straight. His sister, Reyna, is bisexual, and Charlie is gay, and I have no idea what the chance is of a three-fer for being queer, but it can't be all that high.

Can it?

I'm assuming Cam is straight and therefore unavailable, so he's totally my type. Eye roll.

A sharp pain lances through my cheek. I want to call someone, because I need to process what just happened, except I'm not sure I'm coherent enough to make sense. I hurt in weird places. But I hit the hands-free anyway and, with clammy fingers, call the first number I get to in alphabetical order.

Thankfully, Alden picks up fast. He's become one of my good friends over the course of the past few months. He's the newish bookkeeper at Weston & Ramirez, where I've worked for eight years. In fact, I was the first employee—the founders, Noah Weston and August Ramirez, hired me while I was still in high school.

"Hey," I say, struggling with how to begin.

"What's wrong?" Alden asks.

I lick my bruised lips. "How did you know something's wrong? I mean, it is, but ..."

"I can tell by your voice," he says. "Are you okay?"

He's such a sweetie. I guess I do sound defeated. I'm only just now getting my limbs to stop shaking and the dizziness to go away. "I am now. Or I will be."

"What happened?"

"So, you know Evan?"

"I haven't met him."

"So, you know how I was dating that guy, Evan?" My voice sounds falsely cheerful, even to me.

"Was? Uh-oh."

"Yeah, uh-oh. Apparently he didn't tell me that he has a wife and family in New York." I turn right, following Cam through the Valley.

"What?" Alden yelps, and in the background I hear Danny, his boyfriend—and a lawyer at our firm—ask what's wrong.

"Ugh." I stop at a red light behind Cam. "So, I thought I'd finally found a guy who was out of the closet ... but nope. He's only out when he's in LA. He's a talent agent, and I knew he traveled a lot. But he didn't tell me about this whole other life."

"That's terrible!"

"It gets worse. I found out about it, and"—I gulp, feeling the shakes try to start up again—"he got physical. Took some swipes at me."

"Oh my god, are you okay?"

The light turns green, and we take off again. "I'm fine."

"Uh, no. If he hit you, that's not fine. It's battery. Are you going to report it to the police?"

I can hear Danny in the background asking if he needs to go pay someone a visit, and my heart leaps. Some people just go to work. I'm lucky and have ended up working with amazing, supportive people who have become my close friends. I know they have my back.

My instincts tell me not to be a snitch. For one thing, I'm scared of the blowback. Worse, I'm mortified about the whole thing. That I even got involved with such a loser, that Cam had to save me, that he got hurt. I just want to forget about it. I'm much too ashamed to talk about this to anyone who would judge me for my bad decisions.

"I don't know if that's a good idea. It could come back to bite me."

"I'm sure we can protect you," Alden says.

"It's not me who needs protection." Or not primarily me.

"I don't understand."

Poor Alden. I know I'm not making much sense. I try again. "Um, this funny thing happened. You know Charlie's brother Camden?"

"I don't think so."

"You met him at the Fourth of July party."

"Did I? I don't remember."

I smirk, despite my all-over aches. Alden's pretty much totally wrapped up in Danny. It figures he wouldn't notice any other guy, no matter how hot. Because phew. Cam Cooper is as hot as they come.

"Anyhow, Cam was working on a house next door, and he saw me leaving. Maybe he heard some of the commotion, I dunno. He came over, and he kind of, sort of, maybe beat Evan up. A tiny bit."

"What?"

"Cam didn't throw the first punch. That was all Evan."

"Still ..."

"Yeah, still. I'm scared," I admit. "I don't want Evan to come after me. And I don't want him to press charges against Cam. Although I suppose on Cam's side, it was self-defense. Or defense of me. Cam could press charges, too, I guess. I don't know, but he got hurt."

"Oh my god. Is he okay?"

"I don't know. And Evan threatened to sue him—"

"Tell Camden to ask for a lawyer if he gets arrested," Danny calls in the background. "And not say anything else. *Anything*."

I almost shriek. "No one is getting arrested. Cam doesn't need a lawyer—at least I hope he doesn't. Because if Evan called the police, I'd tell the truth about him hitting me because his wife found out about him, and his whole house of cards would come tumbling down. He's got a rep to protect."

"Wait," Alden says. "Didn't you just move in with Evan?"

"Yeah. So that's another issue. Cam is taking me back to his house, and I'm going to crash in his guest room—or, rather, pool house—for a day or two until I figure out where I'm going to go next."

"Well, that's nice of him. Sounds like him being there was oddly lucky."

"Not for his ankle."

"What?"

I explain how Cam twisted his ankle badly, but he doesn't want to go get it checked out.

"That sucks," Alden says. "This is so horrible."

"I know." I pause and suck on my lip, tasting the metallic tang of blood. It hurts from where Evan hit it. "There is a small silver lining. I don't think I've ever had anyone stick up for me the way he did." And there were times in the past when I needed it.

"Never?"

"Not counting the support we have in the office. But that's

different." I sigh and inspect my lip in the rearview mirror. Catching a glimpse of the dark brown-purple bruise forming on my cheek, I grimace. "So, yeah. I'm in the market for a new place to live."

"And a new boyfriend?"

"No. I don't think I want a new boyfriend anytime soon. I just can't seem to get it right."

"You will someday." Alden's quiet assurance makes me feel better.

"I think we're getting close to his house," I say, noticing Cam turning into a subdivision of older tract homes. They're mostly tidy, and the properties seem kept up to date. "I'll talk with you later."

"Keep us posted, please. Want me to keep it to myself, or is it okay to tell people you're having issues?"

"I'd rather not tell the whole world, but they'll know right away when they see my face."

I can hear Alden suck in a sharp breath. "Do *you* need to go get medical care?"

"No. I'm fine."

"Okay," he says slowly. "If you say so. If we can do something to help, please let us know."

We. Us. He means him and Danny. That's what happens when you're part of a stable couple. You become a unit. I only wish I had an "us." Until a little while ago, I thought I did.

I swallow. "Thanks. I'm sure I'll be fine."

We slow down, and Cam signals again. "Thanks, Alden. We're here. I'll talk with you later?"

"Anytime."

I hang up and take a deep breath. Although I'm still upset about Evan, the drive here has at least made it so I'm not trembling anymore.

Cam pulls into the driveway of a medium-sized tract home, then tenses in pain the second he sets his foot on the ground. I park next to him and scurry over, ignoring the hot concrete under my feet. "Hey," I say. "Do you want me to go to the store and get you some crutches?"

He shakes his head. "No. It's fine. I'll wrap it up after I show you around. Come on."

"Stubborn man," I mutter. While I'll let him give me a tour, I already know what his pool house looks like, since I saw his videos on the build. "Fine." I go back to my car and grab some flip-flops from my duffel bag while Cam waits for me by his truck. At Evan's, I'd run into our bedroom and barricaded the door while I threw clothes, shoes, and personal papers, along with a few of my toiletries, into the first bags I could find. I left behind the rest of my clothes, as well as things like my craft supplies, which I'll have to get later. Or never. I take one bag with me for now but leave a hand free just in case Cam stumbles.

Cam gestures at his front door. "Um, the house is a construction zone, so let me take you around the side. You can stay and have free rein of the place until you find something else. You won't even have to see me if you don't want to."

"But what if I want to see you?" Shit, that sounded flirty.

He just chuckles. "I guess we can work something out."

We pass through a gate and go down a landscaped path along the left side of the house. Cam is limping and moving very gingerly, but I'm not going to annoy him by repeating my offer of help.

The large backyard opens up to a medium-sized swimming pool and a pool house at the far end of the lot. It's all super nice, and I recognize some of the projects from the Ad/VICE channel: A fire feature near the pool. A sculptural fountain. An outdoor kitchen.

We go to the pool house, and Cam opens it up. I try to act surprised at the adorable unit. There's a bright, cozy bedroom with a sleek bathroom. While the building is a functional pool house that has towel storage, an outdoor shower, and a changing room, with the bedroom setup, it feels more like a studio apartment, with even a tiny fridge and microwave. The design is very airy and light, and it feels immediately soothing. Like a home.

Cam kind of props himself up against the doorway and fiddles with his keychain. "Here's the key. You can come and go as you like, but the house is basically uninhabitable, so I'd advise staying in here."

"I'm sure you're exaggerating."

Cam shakes his head and scratches the back of his neck. "I'm not." He looks down at his foot. "Um, I'd help you bring your other bags in, but ..."

I wave my hand. "I can handle it. It's not much. And I need to go to the store, since I'm not totally sure what toiletries I grabbed —and I have no food, though right now I don't have much of an appetite. It's okay, I got this."

"You sure?"

"Yeah, it's no problem." On impulse, before Cam can turn and limp away, I bound over to him and hug him around his waist, careful not to pull him onto his bad foot. He smells like hard work and breezy sunshine, and his muscular torso feels amazing. He tenses, then returns the hug, wrapping a big bicep around me. "Thanks," I whisper.

He lets go of me and ruffles my hair. "You're welcome. Get settled. I'll find some ice and bring you the first aid kit."

Rather than embarrass him by watching him slowly make his way to the house, I head back to my car to get the rest of my things.

* * *

"So, in summary, Camden Cooper not only ran to my rescue but is also my new landlord," I say to Noah the following morning at work, as we get our coffees in the break room.

Noah's tall, with light hair and blue eyes, and he's rocking a tailored dark gray suit. He grins and sips his coffee, then starts fixing another cup. I know who that's for—his new husband and longtime best friend, August. He studies my face. "You sure you're okay?"

"I took some meds. It's just a bruise." A few pain relievers and some ice helped a lot. And I'm wearing makeup to cover most of what's left.

The stuff you can't see—words, insults, the silent treatment—hurts more than any punch, anyway. I learned that growing up.

"Cam coming to save you sounds kind of romantic," Noah says.

"Yeah." I sigh. "But he's straight."

"Ah, then he's your type."

I huff, but I smile, too. Noah knows me well. "Since when did you get so sassy?"

"Since he married me." August walks up behind Noah, wraps his arms around him, and kisses his cheek. Like Noah, August is also tall and wearing a suit. His brown eyes glimmer with mischief.

I can't help my grin. "God, it's good to see you two finally be open and affectionate."

They both smile at me, and I feel a twinge in my heart. I think it might be jealousy? Not sure. All I know is that I want what they have: a loving and supportive relationship that the whole world can see.

"Hey, Shelbs, do you want to plan the holiday party this year?" Noah asks. "Or you and someone else? Demi, maybe?"

"I'm always up for planning a party. What's the budget?"

"I'll email you," he says. "Have fun with it. You can make it family friendly and we can go bowling, or whatever. I know you'll come up with something good."

"Sounds like fun!"

Alden walks in, stows his lunch bag in the fridge, and looks around. He's gotten less shy since he started working here, and he gives us a little wave, his curly mop of hair falling into his eyes as he makes himself a cup of tea.

Demi, our office manager, strides into the room behind him, holding an iPad. She's petite, with black hair and brown eyes. And she seems like she's on a mission. "Now that you're married, do you think you guys will have any changes in your insurance?" she asks Noah and August. "I'm taking a survey for when I talk with our broker. I know open enrollment doesn't start until November, but I have a meeting with her next week."

They look at each other. "I think we can keep it how it is," August says slowly.

"Well, let me look at the rates," Noah says.

August nods and shrugs. "What he said."

"Got it. I'll find out the rates." Demi tilts her head. "In any case, congrats, newlyweds. How do you two like being married? What's different?"

Noah thinks about it for a moment. "It's hard to say. We were so close, and we had so many inside jokes and shared memories already."

"And it's not like you need to get married to have sex anymore," August says. Noah elbows him. "What?" August protests. "It's true."

"I guess that's why so many people don't bother with marriage nowadays," Noah says. "I mean, it has legal consequences, for sure —although with us, since we already jointly owned the law firm, it doesn't feel that much different."

"We were already a couple—just not in the romantic sense— before we knew it." August catches Noah's mock glare and corrects himself. "Before *I* knew it." He gets a kiss from Noah for that.

"But there is *something* different," Noah says slowly. "Otherwise August wouldn't have proposed so many times that I lost count. And I wouldn't have wanted him to."

I count on my fingers. "So marriage is inside jokes, shared memories, sex, and legal consequences. Good to know."

Everyone laughs. "I suppose that's one definition," Noah says.

"I think it's also having someone to stick up for you. Oh, and love. You know, the big reason people get married."

Love. That would be nice.

"That's cool," Demi says. "For now, marriage means filling out health insurance forms."

"And thank you for wrangling our benefits," Noah says. He hands August a cup of coffee, and they leave while Demi does something on the iPad.

I'm realizing how easy I have it, compared to Cam and anyone else without good benefits. A few clicks, and I'm covered.

Thinking about Cam makes me worry. I'm hoping his ankle isn't as bad as it seems—but he was in a lot of pain last night, even if he was trying to hide it. When he came by my room to give me ointment and ice, I didn't miss his grimace every time he moved.

"Okay." Demi turns to me and Alden. "What about you two? Any changes?" Alden looks at her questioningly, and she clarifies, "In your insurance."

"I don't think so," I say.

"Can you only change health insurance at the end of the year?" Alden asks.

"If you have a life change, like you have a kid or get married, you can change it immediately. But otherwise, our policies require waiting until open enrollment."

"No kids, not married, no changes," I say.

"Same," Alden says. Although his ears pink.

"What is this?" I ask teasingly. "What are you not telling us?"

"I was just thinking about marriage, that's all." Alden didn't notice Danny, his tall, dark, and handsome boyfriend, walk in behind him, followed by another attorney, Sam Stone. Like the rest of the lawyers, Danny's in a sharp suit, and he has a precise fade haircut. Sam's wearing a bow tie. He's very blond and dating a very famous rock star, Julian Hill.

"Do you want to get married?" I ask Alden, holding in my smirk. Danny raises an eyebrow, and he and Sam exchange looks.

Alden nods. "Yeah, I think I do. Someday."

"That so?" Danny asks, and Alden jumps. I put a hand over my mouth to stifle a laugh, and Sam and Demi grin.

"Sheesh, you startled me," Alden says.

"Sorry," Danny says, not sounding at all sorry. He gives Alden a quick kiss. "Should we be talking about this marriage thing?"

"Um," Alden stammers. "No? Yes? I don't know."

Danny smiles at him. "How about when you're ready for it?"

"Sounds good to me. I mean, okay. Yes. That is, I'm not saying yes to marriage right now. I would, though. I think. Oh, god ..." Alden turns bright red.

Danny wraps an arm around Alden's shoulders and steers him out of the room, whispering in his ear.

Demi, Sam, and I look at each other in amusement. "Those two are super cute together," she says.

"I know. I'm jealous." I turn to Sam. "Is Julian working on another album?"

"He is. It's amazing." He looks wistful.

"What about you?" Demi asks me. "Anyone special in your life?"

"Not really. Evan and I broke up."

That's an understatement, but I don't have to have everyone all in my business right away. Even if they're good people.

"Sorry to hear that. And sorry to bring it up." She shakes her head. "I can't keep up with you."

"My advice is, don't even try," I say with a grin.

CHAPTER 3

Camden

After limping around the house last night, I've canceled all my plans and given up attempting to work for the next few days. Since I'm my own boss and don't have any employees under my license, I reschedule what I can, and what I can't, I pass on to other contractors.

I've also taken more over-the-counter meds than are recommended. I'm ignoring the color of my ankle. And the size of the swelling.

It's not just the pain that's bothering me, or the fact that I'm missing work. I'm starting to worry that there's something wrong with my ankle that isn't going to be fixed with ice, elevating it, and an overdose of Aleve. Which makes me stress about not being able to do things I love. For starters, I'm thinking this means I'm missing out on the upcoming ski season. From there, I start spiraling into a panic where I'm imagining that I'll never walk again, though I know that's irrational.

To turn off that line of doomsday scenarios, I turn on the television to numb my mind along with my ankle.

Likely because Shelby told them, both my brother and sister know about the injury and called me first thing this morning, asking how I'm doing. Reyna even leaves work midday to brave nine miles of traffic and bring me lunch. I tell her that she doesn't have to worry, that I can order delivery, but she won't hear it.

When she walks in, she finds me on the couch watching *Building Off the Grid*, my leg propped up on the coffee table. Her face falls as she sets my lunch down before me. She's wearing a power suit; guess she had to go to court today.

I'm from a family of overachievers. I'm the outlier among my siblings: older, less accomplished, and straight.

"How is your ankle feeling?" Reyna asks.

"It's fine." I cough, muting the TV. My ankle is still pretty fucked up, but she doesn't need to know that. It's such an embarrassing injury. "I just stepped on it wrong."

She seems to read through me, though, because she narrows her eyes. "Uh-huh. And what did the doctor say?"

I look away. "Nothing."

"What do you mean, nothing?"

"I mean a doctor hasn't seen it yet."

Reyna gasps and puts a hand on her hip. "Are you serious? What the hell, Camden? Go to the doctor. I can drive you."

"It's fine."

"It's clearly not fine if you're barely able to walk. Shelby said you seemed to be in a lot of pain."

"Animals in the wild heal without going to the doctor. Why can't I?"

"I don't even want to dignify that with a response." She pauses. "Is it because you're scared of the doctor?"

I scoff. I lean forward and open the bag, sniffing gratefully. She brought my favorite meatball sub. "No."

"Do you even *have* a regular doctor?"

"No."

Reyna takes a step closer, her high heels clicking on my concrete floor. "What about health insurance? Do you have health insurance?"

"No," I mutter. "I don't. Stop cross-examining me."

"Shit." She starts pacing. "If you need money—"

"Don't even go there. I'm not borrowing money from you. Or Mom and Dad. I'm in enough debt as it is."

"Prideful so-and-so."

"Maybe. Don't care. And I know what the doctor's going to say. They're going to tell me I need surgery or to get X-rays or go to a specialist. And order all kinds of tests I can't pay for."

"*Don't want* to pay for."

"You know I've sunk all my money into the house. Cash is low right now"—especially given the extra expenses I had last year—"and if I have to ride this injury out, I'm not sure how I'm going to make more. I can't exactly get unemployment when I've been self-employed." I'm a licensed Class B general contractor. I sub out work I can't do or hire laborers. But everything I had lined up in the foreseeable future requires me to be there.

"Shit. Until you get better, do you have any way of making money? You could rent out the pool house."

"That's what it's set up for, yeah. But not right now. Shelby's in there, and I'm not going to charge him. I told him he could stay as long as he needs to, to get himself back on his feet, and I meant it. I'll deal." The Airbnb listing I planned can wait.

Reyna sighs. "It's not easy, is it?"

"What?"

"Adulting."

I shake my head, feeling defeated. It's not like I *want* to avoid medical treatment, but I'm not sure what the right thing to do is.

"Let me at least take you to urgent care," she begs, and I relent. How expensive can one appointment be?

Four hours later, it's as bad as I thought—in every respect. Eight hundred and seventy-three dollars buys me the information that I somehow managed to fracture my ankle in two places. The doctor outlines treatment, and ... I stop listening before she gets to the total. It's more money than I have, that's for sure.

I feel sick to my stomach. When I limp out with Reyna, she gives me a sympathetic smile.

"Talk with Shelby," she suggests. "You don't have to kick him out, but maybe he does have somewhere else he could stay, so you could get that place rented out after all. And who knows—he always has good ideas for the office. He's the one who implemented the canned food drive and the tree planting to celebrate the firm's anniversary. Maybe he'll come up with some creative solution to help your sorry ass."

"Thanks," I say. "I'm glad I'm up there with trees and cans."

She leans over and gives my shoulder a gentle shove. "You know what I mean." Then her expression turns serious. "I just want you to get better, okay? A girl's big brother shouldn't be down for the count. He's supposed to be there for her."

"Oh, so we're moving on to guilt trips now?"

"Whatever I can do to motivate you to get yourself in gear, I'm going to do."

* * *

In the evening, I see the lights turn on in the pool house when Shelby returns. I'm not feeling like I can get up and turn on my own lights, so I sit here in the dark like a weirdo.

A few minutes later, though, there's a rap on my sliding glass door, and then it opens. "Okay for me to come in?" Shelby calls.

"Sure." My voice sounds creaky.

"Why are you sitting in the dark—" He cuts himself off. "Because you don't want to get up. I gotcha." He turns on the light, and he can't hide his sharp inhale.

"Yeah, I know," I say. "It's a work in progress."

It's a wreck, is what it is. A lot of my house is down to the studs, and there's no ceiling, because I've been redoing the duct-work. The place is a disaster zone. In fact, some disaster zones might look better.

He's still dressed for work, much more put together than he was yesterday. I inspect his face. He seems to not have too much bruising, although I suspect he's wearing makeup to cover it up.

"How can you live in here?" Shelby gestures around, looking confused.

I shrug. "My bedroom and bathroom are okay. And I have a fridge, a microwave, and a hot plate. And a dishwasher."

He lifts up his hands. "Oh my god, Camden. This isn't safe."

"I'm a contractor. I know how to be on a construction site."

"But you don't need to live in one." I'm vaguely expecting him to shake a finger at me, though he doesn't.

"Things are always a little uncomfortable while they're in process. When it's done, it will be great."

When I get the money to finish it.

When I can work again to make the money.

When my ankle is healed enough to walk on.

"How are you feeling?"

"Not great," I admit. "I went to urgent care," I add, "and I can't afford the treatment they outlined except the recommendation of keeping off it."

"Is it really that bad?"

I swallow hard. "They told me it's twelve weeks until I can put weight on that foot. It's fractured in two places."

"Twelve weeks?" He inhales sharply, then tilts his head and squints at me. "Did you at least get crutches while you were out?"

I shake my head. By the time I left the doctor's, all I wanted was to go home and lick my wounds.

Shelby holds up his hand. "Don't go anywhere." He spins on his heel.

"Where am I going to go?" I mutter at his retreating back.

When he returns forty-five minutes later with a rented pair of crutches from a medical supply store, along with a boot, I get a weird feeling in my stomach that has nothing to do with what I last ate. He's laden with bags from a grocery store and a restaurant as well.

"Thank you," I say, and my voice sounds husky.

"You're welcome," he says with brisk efficiency. "I also brought you some Gatorade and soup. It's Greek lemon chicken, and there's some pita bread, too. I know you're not *that* kind of sick, but we all want hydration when we're feeling bad." He hands me the container of soup, a plastic spoon, and a warm paper bag that smells heavenly, then sets the Gatorade on the coffee table. He gestures at my wrapped ankle. "Having an untreated fracture can't be good for you. You're going to end up like that giraffe with the crooked neck." He moves to the kitchen, or what will eventually be the kitchen, and starts putting some boxes of cereal and pasta on the counter and cut-up fruit in the fridge.

I wrinkle my nose. "What are you talking about?"

"When I was a little kid, I went to the Santa Barbara Zoo, and there was a giraffe with a crooked neck. I think it got hurt and never healed properly. It lived a long time, but still ... I don't want you to have any issues with walking. Especially since you use your body for work."

A jolt of panic tears through my body faster than I can hide it, and I can tell Shelby sees. "I don't want problems like that, either," I say, trying to keep my voice steady, "but it's tens of thousands of dollars that I don't have right now. All because I stepped wrong."

Shelby shifts his weight. "But isn't your health priceless?"

"Yeah, but ... I guess I'm just hoping it heals on its own."

"What if it doesn't, though? And besides, you should have health insurance in general. Someone needs to check your blood pressure and whatever else." Now he's really getting going. "I'm going to start looking for low-cost health insurance for you."

"You don't have to do that."

He bites his lip, then grimaces. So he *is* still hurting where Evan hit him, which makes me want to do things to put his ex in as much pain as I'm in. Or more. "Don't be so stubborn. You know there are options."

"I don't know. Maybe. But won't they require a physical or have a waiting period? And this is now a preexisting condition, so I don't know if it would be covered."

"I wish I could just get you on my insurance," Shelby says. "It covers preexisting conditions. We have a terrific plan. Noah and August made sure of it. I think it's because they do so many extreme sports, they wanted to make sure they were covered for everything imaginable—and because they're such good guys, they wanted all their employees to have the same benefit."

"That does sound nice."

"It's going to be open enrollment in the fall ..."

"But I'm not your dependent or part of your family."

"Maybe you could sign up through Reyna or Charlie."

"I don't think you can include siblings. I'm not sure. I think it's only spouses and children."

"Spouses?" Shelby looks me straight in the eye. "Then marry me."

CHAPTER 4

Shelby

Camden gapes at me.

"What?" I say, defensively. "If you were my spouse, you'd have health insurance."

He blinks. "You know I'm straight, right?"

"I didn't mean we have to have sex. Or is it that you don't like the idea—"

"I'll cut you off right there," he says. "Of course I'm a total ally. That's not the issue. I just didn't think you'd want to be married to a straight guy, on top of me being someone you barely know. What if you meet someone? How will you explain ..." Cam gestures between us.

I put a hand on my hip. "It's not like they're lining up around the block to date me." I scrub my face. "Look, no pressure. But if we get married, we can enroll you right away and you can get your injury treated. And then in a few months, when you're healed and you can get your own health insurance, we can divorce. By the new year, we'll have gone our separate ways."

Cam sighs and pinches his nose. "I can't believe I'm actually contemplating saying yes to this, but, to be totally candid, I'm not doing so well. When the doctor told me it was fractured, you know, it wasn't a surprise. I figured as much. I broke an arm as a kid, and this is about the same level of pain."

"I'm so sorry."

He waves away my concern. "It wasn't your fault." Which I suppose is true, but it's also true that if not for me, he wouldn't have a broken ankle right now. "Anyway," he says, "if we do this, what are we going to tell people? I mean, you're still going to want to date, right? I guess we can say we're in an open relationship." He studies me.

"I ... Hmm. No. After Evan, I'm taking an extended break from dating."

"Okay, then if the marriage isn't going to last long anyhow, we're probably good on that count. But there's more than that to consider. When you get married, there are rules about assets and who owns what."

"I don't have any assets other than a bank account that pretty much covers my monthly bills, so we don't need a prenup. At least not for me. I won't ask for anything of yours, but I know a lawyer or two—and so do you—if you want to have them draft something."

Cam chuckles mirthlessly. "I'm mortgaged to the hilt." Then he closes his eyes and shakes his head. "I can't believe I'm actually considering this. Okay, so no prenup. But I'll definitely pay for the increase in your insurance premium."

"Or just count it as my rent? I mean, the cost difference has to be cheaper than rent, so maybe I'm getting a bargain. I don't mind paying additional rent over that."

"No," he says. "Let me see how much you're talking about, but I'm sure whatever it costs is fine as rent. And you can stay as long as you need to."

My heart starts to beat a little faster. Are we doing what I think we're doing? I mean, it was my idea, but I always thought that getting married would be a bigger deal than calmly discussing it in the living room with someone I'm not even dating.

Something inside me aches for Cam. He must really be in a lot of pain. I can't see him agreeing to an arrangement like this unless he were desperate. I wish I could reassure him that it'll be okay. I'm happy to help him, and it doesn't have to mean anything. We can do this as long as we need to, and when it's done, it's done.

I know a thing or two about someone keeping a promise just long enough to satisfy an obligation. Talk to my mother. Or, more to the point, look at the card in the bottom of the pool house dresser drawer that reminds me not to get my hopes up.

"I'm good with it," I say. "With or without an agreement. I'll marry you. Let's go."

"Whoa," he says, holding up his hand. "Don't you want to, I don't know, put on a suit or something? I think we should observe *some* of the traditions, don't you?" Then he mutters something I don't catch.

The specifics of a ceremony aren't something I've ever really considered, mostly because it seemed premature until I was with someone I wanted to marry. "You tell me," I say. "If you want to have the full ceremony, let's do it." Then I grin. "Camden Cooper, will you marry me?"

He laughs. "Um, I think yes. Just let me make sure we have everything we need for the paperwork at the clerk's office. Or wherever it is we're going to say our vows."

"So romantic." I giggle. "I'll reserve us a spot."

He gives me a sweet smile, and something inside me shifts, a warmth infusing my body. Yeah, okay. I don't know him that well, but he's ... husband material. Protective, communicative, caring. I know his brother and sister, and I'm pretty sure he's good people, like them.

I pull out my phone and make an appointment for tomorrow at the nearest clerk's office. Then I look up at him. "So the deal is, we get married, and I'll put you on my insurance plan until you heal. I'll stay here until I find another place, and I'll help you find your own insurance, too. When we're all set, we'll get divorced."

"Sounds like a plan," Cam says.

While I'm happy to be helping him, I can't help feeling a heavy weight in my stomach as we sketch out the demise of our union. But we're not in a relationship. Like, at all. We aren't even more than acquaintances. I'm not sure what my heart is reacting to—maybe some combination of my unrequited crush on Cam and the disappointment of learning what a jerkwad Evan was. Still, I have to remember that this marriage is to get Cam health insurance, nothing more. I smile. "Cool. As soon as we're legal, I'll ask Demi in the office to add you to my insurance, and then you can get that ankle taken care of."

"So should we get dressed up and go over to the clerk's office tomorrow?" Cam asks. "What's your ring size? Do you know what kind of ring you want?"

All of a sudden, this blurt of mine is becoming real. And while I know I could stop this train, I don't really want to. Most importantly, because I want to help Cam. But also ... I'm letting myself get caught up in this fantasy. That I can have a wedding day with a gorgeous guy.

I need to keep things in perspective. We'll just sign some papers and exchange I-dos. No romance involved.

"We don't need rings," I say.

He clucks his tongue. "If we're going to do this, we're going to do it right. I don't want your insurance company coming after you because we weren't really married, and rings are a symbol of marriage. Besides, we should let everyone know you're off the market." He falters. "So to speak. If you're good with that."

"Yes," I croak. "I'm good with that."

I may need therapy afterward, but for now I'm good with being legally married to a hot, straight guy so he can have health insurance to fix his ankle—which he hurt while saving me from my evil ex.

Sounds totally normal.

Part of me wonders, though, if I'll ever be able to touch my future husband. I'm talking even hold his hand, let alone kiss him. Odds are that's a fantasy that's never going to come true.

Still, if this is the worst thing that I get myself involved in, I can't complain. It's not every day you get engaged.

He smiles at me, and wow, his smile is nice: straight teeth and an unreserved expression. "This is the most ridiculous thing I've ever done, but I'm really grateful to you." He shifts, and then he looks at his foot and sucks in his lip, wincing in pain.

Enough is enough. "Then we're getting married. Tomorrow."

* * *

"Are you sure this is a good idea?" Alden asks me the next morning at work, after I explain the plan for the third time.

"No, I'm not sure of anything. But I'm rolling with it." I'm hit with inspiration. "Want to come? We're going at one. You can take a long lunch and be my best man."

Alden's eyes light up. "Really?"

"Yeah, of course."

"I'd love to."

I bite my lip. "I need to go buy something better to wear—when I dashed out of Evan's place, I didn't think about dressing for a wedding. I'm going to see if Noah will let me have more time. Want to go shopping with me?"

"Sure. Do you think I should wear my suit jacket to the ceremony?" Alden asks. "I'll need to get it from my office." He's so cute, always wondering what he should wear. Danny got him to buy clothes that fit him better and to be brave enough to wear the things that he likes. Now Alden's a bit of a clotheshorse. As am I.

"If you want to," I say. My knee-jerk reaction was to say he should dress up, since I'm only getting married once ... except, I guess, I hope that's not true. I still want to meet the right guy and get married for real someday. After Cam and I get divorced.

Gosh, my life is getting confusing.

After explaining to Noah what I'm doing—and waiting while Noah processes his shock—I get half the day off with support staff covering the front desk. He lets Alden take time off, too, and we head out the door to my car.

"But what's going to happen after he gets his ankle taken care of?" Alden asks while we drive to some nearby boutique he's been to before. "You're just going to be friends?"

"To tell you the truth, we're barely friends right now. I guess, yeah, we'll take care of the legal stuff and then go back to being acquaintances." I shrug. "It'll be okay."

"If you say so," Alden says. "I worry about you, you know? You go around helping everyone else. But do you ever take care of you? This is a big thing to do for someone else."

"I'm doing this for me, too. I get a place to stay until I get back on my feet, without feeling like I'm taking advantage. Besides, he helped me and got hurt in the process, so I feel like it will erase a debt to him. I like doing nice things for people, anyway."

"And that makes you feel good?"

I nod.

"Okay, then. I understand that." He smiles.

This is why I like Alden. He doesn't try to push me into some preconceived mold of who he thinks I should be. He lets me be who I am.

I have butterflies in my stomach, I can't lie. Because even if it's a marriage of convenience. Even if Cam is straight. Even if I don't really know him.

I'm *getting married*.

And that's a big deal. I know it's a big deal. I keep trying to minimize it inside my head, but I shouldn't.

Part of me wonders if I should tell my parents. Probably not. My mom doesn't really have time for me, and I don't know what my dad is up to.

Thinking about my parents is never a good idea. It reminds me that I was a burden to them. And from there it's only a short step to thinking I don't want to be a burden to my new husband.

Alden sees my crestfallen look. "For someone who's getting married, you're pretty subdued."

"I'm happy," I insist. "I guess I just wish it were for real. But it's never going to be. I should be grateful for what I've been given. And I'm really happy to be able to help Camden out. He helped me out."

"He seems like a super nice guy," Alden says. "I agree. You could do much worse."

I snort. "Like his brother?" Charlie has the rep of being kind of a jerk, but there's a mushiness inside him.

"Hey. Charlie is Danny's best friend!"

"True. But he's an acquired taste."

Cam, though. Cam seems like he's something else entirely.

Something *straight* else, I remind myself. Not that I'm repeating any damned patterns here. Patterns I thought I was breaking with Evan.

How wrong I was.

Alden and I find street parking not far from the clothing store. He stops short as we walk from my car and pulls out his phone, taking a picture of the concrete.

"What are you doing?" I ask.

"This is where Danny and I had our first kiss. It was my first kiss *ever*."

"Aww," I say. It's impossible not to be happy for Alden and Danny. They're an adorable couple. At the same time, I'm jealous —not about Alden having his first kiss here, but because he has a real boyfriend to share memories with. I always wanted that—to have *things* together, experiences that we developed as a couple over time. Little jokes and places we went together.

I'm not going to get that in this marriage. I'll be lucky if I get a hug sometimes.

The boutique ends up having reasonable prices, and I quickly find a blue suit that will work, with a light blue and pink floral print shirt and a pastel tie. I love it. I feel sharp in it.

And darn it, even if we're only getting married so Cam can get his ankle fixed, I want to look and feel good. I leave the store wearing my new suit and head to the clerk's office.

For my wedding.

CHAPTER 5
Camden

A few minutes after eleven o'clock, Charlie pulls up in front of the house. I'm waiting on the sidewalk, leaning on my crutches. The day is already hot, and sweat trickles down the back of my neck under my collar. He rolls down the window. "Where are we going?" he asks. "And why are you all dressed up?"

I clear my throat and open the back passenger door to put my crutches in. All I told my brother was that I needed to do a few errands this morning. Since he's a lawyer, he makes his own schedule, and lucky for me, he didn't have anything time-sensitive on his calendar today. "Um. A florist, Costco, and the county clerk's office. I'm wearing a suit because I'm getting married to your receptionist."

"What the hell?" he yelps as I hop to the front seat and get in. Thankfully, the car is air-conditioned.

I point down the street. "Go that way."

Charlie gives me a hard look as I buckle up. "Camden. What the actual fuck are you doing today?"

"I'm getting married to Shelby Borchard at one."

His jaw drops. "There are so many things wrong with that

sentence, I don't even know where to start. For example, I wasn't aware you two knew each other."

While it's the oldest brother's prerogative to be as aloof and mysterious as possible, I decide to put Charlie out of his misery. "We don't, really. It's a long story, but I need health insurance, so he's going to put me on his plan."

"Is your ankle that bad?" He peers down to inspect my injury, but it's wrapped up, and I'm wearing the boot Shelby brought me over my slacks.

I cross my arms. "Yes. It's fractured in two places."

Charlie blanches, then shakes his head. "Okay. But marriage? After last year? That's a little sudden."

I glare. "This has nothing to do with that."

"Do you even like him? Are you even bi?"

"Sure, I like him, but no, I'm not. This is just on paper. He needs a place to stay for a while, and I need a doctor." I sigh and scrub my face. "Actually, I'm panicking because I might need surgery and months of PT, so I need to get going on that as soon as possible."

"And your only solution was to marry him?"

"No, it isn't the only solution, but it's a cheap, fast, and easy one. I can help him out, too." It sounds flimsy, even to my own ears.

Because getting insurance isn't the only reason I'm doing this. I can't explain the protective feelings I have about Shelby. I want him to have a safe place to stay, and I feel like if I marry him, I'll be able to keep him away from bad relationships for a while, even if he says he doesn't want to date anyway. I don't like knowing that his ex hurt him, and if I can keep Shelby close and guard him, I will. Once, you know, my ankle is fixed.

On top of that, I can't say I ever imagined someone would ask *me* to marry *them*. The time I asked someone ... that didn't end up so well.

When Shelby proposed to me, even though I knew it was for practical reasons, I was flattered.

Charlie is giving me a searching look. Then he puts the car in drive and takes off.

"What?" I ask, defensive.

"I don't understand what's going on in that head of yours. You're the straight sibling. That's your job."

"I can still do that and be married to a guy."

"Tell that to the outside world."

"The outside world doesn't matter," I insist.

Charlie grunts. "I have to say that marrying for health insurance is the least romantic reason I've ever heard."

I shrug. "I'm not romantic." Not anymore. "And I don't have a problem with marrying a guy. You should know better than that."

"I didn't say you did. I think it's very ill thought out, but whatever. If this is how you choose to solve problems, then so be it."

I roll my eyes. "Thanks for your vote of confidence."

"You know you never need my approval." He studies me again briefly at a red light, then goes back to driving. "Still ... you sure you're going to be okay? After Leah?"

"I'm fine," I snap.

"Okay, okay, I get it. We don't talk about her. We'll focus on this wedding." Charlie's lips curve in a sly grin. "Do you need a witness?"

"Sure," I say. "Hell, come be my best man."

"What were you going to have me do? Wait in the car?"

"Nah. You can come in."

He laughs. "I thought I was just driving you someplace. This is hilarious. Should I film you for Ad/VICE?"

"No."

"Why not? You'd get the followers' hopes up that you're going to have some romance with a cute guy."

I shake my head. "This is private. But it's okay if you take some photos."

"Did you tell Reyna?"

"No. Yesterday she told me she had court today, so I didn't ask her." I also didn't want the earful I'm sure to get when she learns about this.

"What are Mom and Dad going to say?"

"Mom and Dad aren't going to say anything, because they're not going to find out. This is *temporary*. Until I get healed, and then probably a little bit longer—until we get settled. That's it."

"Well, you already know some divorce attorneys," he says wryly.

I sigh. "I know." I hate the thought of getting a divorce. I realize they're very common, but our folks are still together, and I'd always imagined that when I got married, it would be for keeps—someone of my own to love forever.

Oh well. I have to be practical. Shelby's doing me a big favor with the insurance coverage, and it's not like he's getting in the way of me dating someone else. I've been doing fine on my own since Leah walked out on me, so another few months that way shouldn't be a big deal. I just hope Shelby won't end up regretting it—he's cute and sweet, and he could probably find a real boyfriend in a second if he wanted to. Someone a million times better than that jackass Evan.

Too bad Shelby and I can't be a couple for real. It would make things a lot simpler, but men have never been on my dance card, as it were. I mean, I've thought about it before. I even spent a day in high school—after Charlie came out—wondering if I, too, was gay. But none of the guys there did it for me. The female cheerleaders? Yeah, they did. So I figured I was straight, and that was that.

Then there was the time I accidentally walked in on a friend of Charlie's doing the nasty with another guy at one of Charlie's college parties. I initially reacted like any straight guy, wanting to disinfect my eyeballs. But after I got my thoughts under control, I realized that they'd sounded like they were having a good time, and I wasn't opposed to having a good time.

Over the years, I've attended a ton of LGBT+ events with my siblings, but I haven't been tempted by anyone other than women.

Still, I know that sexuality is fluid. A spectrum. There aren't painted lines that delineate who you like and what you are. People try to put you in boxes that don't really exist. I don't have any hang-ups about the idea of having a romantic or sexual relationship with a man.

But I'm pretty sure I'm straight. And I'm pretty sure that in this instance, it doesn't matter. Shelby finds me convenient—I saved his ass, twice, and now he's saving mine. That's all.

This isn't like the last time I said "I do." Shelby's not going to leave me at the altar. That was intended to be real. This isn't.

We both know the deal going in.

CHAPTER 6

Camden

"You ready?" Charlie asks as we walk up to the government building. I can't read his expression. Is he happy for me? Feeling sorry? He and I have gone through a lot together, but this has to top the list for weirdness.

After all, it's not every day you get married to someone you barely know.

Or limp to your wedding on crutches.

Or get married to someone of the same sex ... when you're straight.

I scrub my face, the crutches under my armpits holding me up. "Yeah."

This is no big deal, I tell myself. This is just so I can get my body fixed and get back to work. This is so I can survive.

That sounds so mercenary. This is also so a kind guy can get away from his evil ex and have a place to stay. We're both helping each other out.

Right? I don't want this to be one-way. I want to give something back to Shelby.

I'm very aware of the rings in my pocket and the fact that I'm about to say vows to legally commit to Shelby. I picked Costco for the rings because last time I bought a set, I went to the most romantic store I could find. Never again. Shelby told me his size, and I really hope it fits. If not, I guess we can get it resized.

I glance over, and Charlie is studying me.

"What?" I ask churlishly as we make our way to the door.

"Nothing. Nothing at all."

I don't believe him, but I let him drop it and do my best to hurry. We're running a little late.

Running. Ha. No running for me anytime soon. That's why we're here, after all.

When I step into the county building, where it's comfortably cool, I look around for Shelby. I can't help it. How's he doing? Is he okay?

Has he come to his senses and decided to back out?

Is he going to get to the last minute, just like Leah, and say no —leaving me hanging, in a tuxedo, in front of two hundred people wondering what the hell they just witnessed?

I shake my head. No. This isn't the same thing. I'm under no illusion that Shelby's in love with me. Unlike her.

Still, I wonder what he's wearing, what he's thinking. A vain part of me hopes he likes that I got dressed up for him.

As we proceed down the hall, I see two men waiting by the door to the registrar, and my heart leaps. One of them is dark haired and slight, but the other, even shorter, has platinum hair that shines despite the crappy fluorescent lights of a government office. He's wearing a stylish suit that shows off his small build. Shelby is someone I always noticed at company picnics, and I'm proud he's going to be on my arm. And yes, I can't help being relieved that he showed up. I couldn't go through *that* embarrassment twice.

Shelby turns around, sees me, and smiles, and something about that smile loosens a tight place in my chest. My heart starts beating really fast, and for a moment I get worried. Even though I don't have a heart condition.

I'm getting married. To a man. To *this* man.

I may not be into men, but he's really handsome—even with the shiner that he wasn't entirely able to hide with makeup. I could do a lot worse than getting married to Shelby Borchard. I almost *did* do worse last year.

Shelby sees that I'm having issues walking with my crutches and comes running, fussing over me. "Hey," he says. "Can I give you a hand somehow?"

"No." I smile at him, reaching out and squeezing his shoulder. "Thanks, though. You look amazing. That's a great suit."

He swallows and nods. "Um. Thanks. You, too. You clean up really well." His voice sounds unnaturally high. "You remember Alden? He's a friend from work."

"Our bookkeeper," Charlie adds.

As Alden shakes my hand, he looks me over curiously. I school my facial features and move closer to Shelby. Charlie stares at us open-mouthed.

"What?" I hiss, once Shelby has turned back to Alden.

Charlie doesn't answer for a moment. Then he murmurs in my ear, "You're really doing this."

I nod. "What's the big deal?"

He zips his mouth shut, but I can tell he's sputtering inside that marriage is a big deal, and that it's a big deal that I'm getting married to a man, not a woman. But whatever.

My attempt to get married for love failed hard. I'm good with getting married for health insurance.

Still, some part of me wishes it were a real wedding. Some part of me wants that commitment.

Charlie passes over a boutonniere, and I pin it onto Shelby, who looks surprised I thought of it. Then Charlie pins mine on me. We bought what the florist had already made, but thankfully the simple pink rose matches the accents in Shelby's floral-print shirt.

Shelby has already taken the clipboard they give you and filled out a lot of the form in his neat, blocky writing. He hands it to me, and I do my best to finish, ignoring how much my hand is shaking.

I hobble up to the line for the clerk's window with Shelby, where we wait behind a few other couples. Some are dressed up, obviously getting married today, while others are just picking up the license for a later ceremony.

We watch as the clerk comes out from behind the counter, stands before a couple, and has them say vows. The newlyweds exchange rings and kiss, and the room is all smiles and applause.

There's a fluttery feeling in my stomach, and my whole body tingles in anticipation.

Before long, it's our turn. In a way, this feels like losing my virginity. That moment when I was naked, in an empty house, with my girlfriend. We'd talked about doing it and messed around plenty, but actually holding the condom, tearing the foil, and rolling it on made everything seem like, once I did it, there was no turning back.

There's no turning back here, either. Well, let me check. I lean over to whisper into Shelby's ear, my lips brushing his skin. "You still good with this?"

"Yeah," he whispers back, and I see goose bumps rise on the back of his neck. "You?"

"Yeah, I am." With my heart pounding, I hand over the forms, our driver's licenses, and a credit card. Shelby tries to pay, but I insist.

Behind my back, I can feel my brother's eyes boring holes into me. I'm sure he's having a silent "WTF?" conversation with Alden.

"Okay, confirming you're Mr. Camden Cooper?" the clerk asks, looking between us and scanning our identification.

"That's me," I say, swallowing hard. *Moment of truth.* I fuss with my tie, which is hard to do while leaning on crutches. Shelby comes over in front of me to straighten it, and I notice how good he smells. He looks up at me and smiles, and my breath quickens.

"Then you're Mr. Shelby Borchard?" the clerk says.

"I am!" Shelby sounds chipper. Once everything is set, the clerk comes around the counter and has us hold hands off to the side of the office. Alden stands just behind Shelby, while Charlie is next to me. He puts a hand on my shoulder, and it's soothing.

Everyone in the room is looking at us, just the way we were looking at the couples before us.

I regulate my breathing. My ankle hurts, but I set that pain to the side. My cheeks are burning, and my hands are trembling. I'm glad my brother is here. I've set my crutches down and taken hold of Shelby's hands. They're clammy, and I'm trying to warm them up. They're also steadying me.

But then he looks up at me with those liquid brown eyes, and my chest feels light. My pulse races, and my mouth goes dry.

After asking us a few more questions, the clerk begins the ceremony. "Do you, Camden, take this man, Shelby, to be your lawfully wedded husband, in sickness and in health, for richer and for poorer, to have and to hold from this day forward until death do you part?"

"I do," I say, and I squeeze Shelby's hands. He gives me a small, genuine smile.

"Do you, Shelby, take this man, Camden—"

Holy shit, I'm getting married. I don't know why it took this long for it to sink in. Something about that fact makes me giddy, and I want to burst out laughing, but I rein it in. Shelby says, "I do," and I let out the biggest breath. Part of me—the part still traumatized by Leah—worried that he'd say no. I want to hug him for saying yes. For not humiliating me.

"You may exchange rings, if you have them."

"Oh. Right." I pull the two bands out of my pocket, and my fingers tremble all over again.

Reaching over, I again take Shelby's soft, tan hand in my work-roughened one, and my jitters vanish when he looks up at me, an expression of wonder on his face, his eyes brimming with tears. He swallows, and I want to hug him or something.

Instead, I place my ring on his finger.

It looks good there, and this possessive feeling—that Shelby is *mine*—rushes through me, even if our situation is temporary.

For now, at least, he *is* mine.

Shelby slips my ring onto my finger. I'm not used to wearing jewelry, but it feels right. Like it's always been there. And I like being able to give Shelby some stability ... for now.

We hold hands, and I can't tell if he's supporting me while my ankle is busted, or I'm supporting him on this wild adventure. Maybe we're supporting each other.

"... and you may kiss your husband," the clerk says, and I have to keep from doing a double take.

Of course, I knew this was a standard part of the ceremony. Heck, I just watched a couple go through this exact process. And I have no problem kissing Shelby—even in front of an audience—but, like *actually* being married, the reality of it hadn't gone through my brain.

I had no clue how it would feel to have him standing before me —like he belongs with me.

Even if this marriage isn't for real reasons, even if I've never been into guys, I'm not going to chicken out on a kiss. Shelby deserves an amazing one ... not that I'm putting pressure on myself to deliver.

He's more than six inches shorter than me, so I tilt his chin up, then drop my mouth to his. I don't want this to be underwhelming, in case it's our only kiss, so I kiss him for real, at length. Not just a peck, but an active, special kiss. One that claims. I'm trying to be careful of his busted lip, but it looks better today than yesterday, and he doesn't seem to mind.

Our tongues caress each other, and I'm not prepared for how good he tastes or how much I like having his body against mine. I'm not ready for how much I like kissing him.

Electricity shoots up my spine as Shelby kisses me back, and now it's going on a little long. It feels different to kiss a man—rougher, even though his skin is smooth. And it turns me on.

That's weird.

When we finally break apart, a throat clears behind me. It's Charlie, of course, but I don't turn. I glance down at Shelby, and he looks dazed. So I kiss him again, softly. "I'm glad we're married," I whisper. There's applause from the other people in the room. The clerk gives us hearty and seemingly sincere congratulations, then signs the license as officiant. Charlie leans over to sign as witness. My ankle throbs, but I'm feeling great.

I catch Alden's eyes, and he's looking at me speculatively. I suppose kissing Shelby that way wasn't exactly what a straight man would do, but what can I say? I liked it. If I'm honest, it woke my body up, and now I'm wondering if I'll ever get to do it again.

We sit down and wait for certified copies of the license, which is awkward. What do we say to each other now? I can't think of anything, so I hold Shelby's hand, not wanting to let him go. He's my husband, and I feel like I need to take care of him.

When we're handed the papers, we're all smiles. "I want some pictures," Alden says, and we pose for him. I give Charlie my phone, and Shelby gives Alden his, so we have a bunch of pictures for ourselves. I also catch Charlie taking a few shots of me and Shelby with his own phone. I kiss the top of Shelby's head, and Charlie gives me a weird look.

I don't care, because it feels right.

While I want to keep holding Shelby's hand as we walk outside, I have to maneuver the crutches, and he has the envelope with our marriage certificate. I catch him inspecting his ring finger.

"I can go to work right now," he says, "and get you enrolled."

I shake my head. "Today's our wedding day. I think we should at least go out to lunch, don't you? Did you eat yet?"

He looks surprised. He pets the flower on his lapel. "No, not yet. And sure. That sounds nice."

I look at Charlie and Alden, who are having a conversation among themselves without talking.

"Why don't I take Alden back to the office," Charlie says, "and you two lovebirds can have lunch on your own." He smirks, and I want to smack him.

But I'm grateful for some time alone with my new husband.

I go to hobble across the parking lot to Shelby's car, but he puts a hand on my bicep. "Let me drive up and get you. Crutches can make your armpits sore after a while. Don't put too much strain on them."

The fact that I don't argue is a sign of how much my ankle hurts.

Or how much I like the idea of my husband being a support system.

Charlie gives me a big bro hug, and Alden shakes my hand. "Congratulations, you two. I hope this works out well for you."

"Me, too," I say. And I mean it.

CHAPTER 7

Shelby

I walk to my car, trying not to trip because I'm staring at the ring on my finger. The simple platinum band feels both light and heavy at the same time. Comfortable and not. This is going to take some getting used to.

Not the wearing jewelry part. Wearing jewelry *with meaning*.

"Do you, Camden, take this man, Shelby, to be your lawfully wedded husband? To have and to hold from this day forward?"

"I do."

A massive sob threatens to erupt from my chest, but I tamp it down. The emotion still manages to make my eyes leak.

Something about Cam's deep, resonant voice just *did it* for me. I know our union is for clinical reasons, but gosh it felt right in the moment. It felt like Cam could want me for the rest of his life.

Like no one else has.

And that's not a thought I need to encourage. For now, I'm mesmerized by the ring, and when I get in my car, I gaze at my hand on the wheel. I like the way the shiny band looks on my finger and how it feels to be part of a unit. An "us."

I start the car, and when I look in the rearview mirror, I see my kiss-stung lips. *What the hell was up with that?*

Cam kissed me for real. Not some light brush of lips. Kissing like that, if he didn't mean it, would win him an Emmy.

I want to kiss him again. I like the way he tastes, like friendliness and something solid that you can rely on.

Except it's probably going to be our only kiss, and worse, it was just for show.

I give myself a quick talking-to. I'm not getting involved with a straight guy. I'm not repeating that pattern ever again. Cam needs medical care, and we're doing this because it's the best way to obtain it for him. We'll get divorced after he's healed. No biggie.

When I drive up to where he's waiting, I get out and help him put his crutches in the back of my Civic.

"Hey," I say, standing awkwardly and holding the door open while he bends over to get in the car. The cut of his suit pants does nothing to hide his bubble ass. He must have gotten that from squatting and lifting things all day long.

Why does the person I'm married to happen to be so beautiful?

When he settles in, he looks up at me, smiles, and says, "Hey."

I close the door for him and return to the driver's seat. Before we drive off, he reaches over and takes my hand, opening his mouth to say something, but I'm focused on his warmth. During the ceremony, I realized it was the first time I'd held his calloused hands, but they felt steadying.

They still do. "You okay?" he asks.

I give him an unreserved smile. "Totally. Oh my god, we got married!"

"I know." He laughs. "It feels surreal. But I'm glad—I mean, I'm glad it's you." And dammit, there goes my heart again. As usual. "Where do you want to go to lunch? What's your favorite place?"

"I like this old Mexican place that's been around for a hundred years. Noah and August won't care if I have a margarita with lunch. August has bought me drinks himself during work hours in the past."

"Then let's go there," he says. "That sounds good."

My *husband* and I drive to my favorite restaurant and walk in. While we wait for the greeter, Cam props himself up on his crutches so he can hold my hand. He seems strangely good with physical contact with me. Maybe it's because his brother and sister are queer, or maybe he's just a touchy-feely guy. He certainly doesn't seem to have any hang-ups about marrying me.

You'd almost think we were actually a couple.

But of course we're not, so it feels kind of hollow. I look at Camden, all warm smiles and confidence, and I wish our marriage were not just legal, but real. *Sigh*.

"Nice flowers. Is there a special occasion?" the greeter asks, gesturing at our boutonnieres.

"We just got married!" Cam announces.

The greeter perks up and congratulates us. The pride in Cam's tone makes me think either he's a better actor than I imagined or —is it possible?—he likes being married to me. What a concept.

It makes me happy. I'm even more pleased when we get seated at a booth with a semicircular seat. I scoot to the middle, and Cam slides in next to me. We're not touching, but it feels like we're aligned. We study the menus, and the server takes our drink orders.

When the server leaves, I ask, "Do you mind if I call the office to enroll you?"

Cam makes a go-ahead gesture. "Please."

I dial the office. When Demi answers, I say, "I'd like to add my spouse to my health insurance."

"Spouse? What the heck? I thought you just broke up with Evan."

I chuckle. "Ummm. So, I married Camden Cooper, Charlie and Reyna's brother. Kinda suddenly."

Demi inhales sharply. "Wow, that is sudden. Well, you do you. Although ... I thought he was straight."

"Oh, so did he." *Actually, Demi, he still is.*

"Okay, I'll add him. What's his date of birth?"

I freeze for a moment, because I should know this about my husband, right? But I did see it on the form. "It's June ..."

"Twenty-third," Cam supplies. He's scooted closer so he can hear the call, and he dutifully recites all the information she needs. Demi tells me she's going to email me the paperwork to sign in short order, and he'll be added promptly, retroactive to today.

When we hang up, I feel a sense of relief. Cam is going to get the medical care he needs. Even if he didn't have an acute problem, I wouldn't want him to go through life the way he has been. That's just too much of a risk.

Cam has his arm over the back of the seat, and he puts his hand on my shoulder to tug me closer. "Come here," he says. He's still in his dress shirt and tie, as am I—we set our jackets off to the side, carefully draped so as not to crush the roses—and his warm strength feels wonderful. I cuddle up next to him, and he continues, "Thanks so much for doing this. I mean it. You're really amazing."

I want to minimize it. Say that I'm just facilitating his access to health care. But it's starting to feel as if this is more than that. So instead, I say, "Anything for you, hubby."

We sit in silence for a moment, and when our margaritas come, we clink glasses and toast to our wedding. I almost think Cam is going to lean in and kiss me—he has this look on his face, soft eyes and parted lips—but that's ridiculous. So I sip my drink instead.

My phone buzzes with what I think is the DocuSign from Demi, but it's a text from Alden.

ALDEN

Enjoy your wedding night ;)

Not that long ago, Alden was a complete innocent. The fact that he's thinking about my wedding night means that now *I'm* thinking about my wedding night. But there's a big difference between a kiss after marriage vows and having sex.

And now that I think about it, what is Cam going to do while we're married? I'm happy to take a break from dating, after that debacle with Evan, but Cam shouldn't be stuck for months on account of this.

We can talk about it if he wants to see other people, I suppose. I imagine he'd have to do some explaining to any woman he picked up, though, because he seems to be wearing that ring proudly.

I go to put my phone away, but it pings again. I smile at Camden. "Maybe this is the DocuSign?"

Except when I look at the screen, it shows a text.

EVAN

I need to talk to you

I feel the blood drain from my face, and Camden notices. "What is it?"

"Evan," I whisper. "He wants to talk."

Cam bristles. "I don't want him anywhere near you." He pauses and takes a breath. "Sorry, I get all protective. I know you can handle yourself."

"Well, kinda," I admit. "He does scare me."

"Then I stand by my original comment."

"We still need to get the rest of my clothes and stuff."

"Is there anything you can't live without for a few more days?"

I shake my head.

"In that case, what do you think about letting him calm down before you contact him to move your stuff out? And we'll bring a small crew to help, so he can't make any trouble."

"I think that sounds good," I whisper. I settle in for a wedding lunch with my husband, cuddled against him, and try not to think about all the things that could go wrong—on any front.

CHAPTER 8

Camden

Soooo, I married a guy.

Weirdly, it's not the "guy" portion of that sentence that feels strangest. The mind-blowing part is that *I got married*. After all, it didn't go so well the last time.

Shelby and I sit in the restaurant crunching chips and drinking margaritas, and I realize that, for the first time in a long time, I'm content.

"I'm so happy we did this," I tell him. "I know it's a strange situation, but it's not just that I'm relieved to get health insurance —although that's part of it." I shrug. "I guess I'm looking forward to getting to know you better." I stutter. "I mean, not in *that* way." Is that true, though? I shake myself. "I guess I really needed a friend."

Shelby beams at me. "I always like having more friends."

His response makes me irrationally grumpy. I don't want to be lumped in with his other friends. I'm his husband. That's special. I brush the irritation away. "Is there something else you want to do on your wedding day?"

"What, like go to Disneyland?" Shelby's platinum blond hair

55

falls across his forehead. It's usually stuck kind of straight up, but it's starting to droop. I like it this way—softer and looser. Not so tidy. I want to reach out and push it from his eyes.

Instead, I smile at him and shrug. "Maybe. I'm not sure my foot is up for all day at an amusement park, but when it's healed ..."

He claps. "When it's healed, we'll go to Disneyland for our honeymoon."

"You got a deal. Happy wedding day," I whisper, and one-arm hug him. I like the way he feels at my side.

"Happy wedding day." He looks up at me, and I can't help it: I kiss him. It's a sweet, chaste kiss, but I kind of want more. He tastes like tangy, salty alcohol. His lips are cool and soft against mine, and I feel that same zing of pleasure I got when we kissed at the clerk's office. Physical chemistry, I think.

That startles me.

Do I have chemistry with Shelby Borchard? The twitch in my pants sure makes me think I do.

Maybe I just haven't been truly open to what it would be like to be with a guy. Or is it that it's Shelby?

He blinks at me, then puts a finger on his lip.

"I'm sorry," I say quickly. "Did I hurt your mouth? Or ... do you mind if I kiss you?"

"I don't mind, and my lip feels fine," he says. "And in the abstract, I like kissing. A lot. I like kissing *you* a lot ..."

"*But*," I prompt.

"But I didn't think you were into guys. Reyna and Charlie always said you were their straight brother."

I sip my margarita. I want to tell him that I'm not sure what I am, but I also don't want to lead him on. "I've never been with a guy before, but I like kissing you. I guess I'm ... curious."

His face falls, and I rewind to consider what I just said. I'm not sure what's wrong with saying how I feel. "Hey," I say. "What is it?"

Shelby shakes his head and sighs. "I think we may need some rules."

Something about his tone makes my heartbeat race. "Oh?"

"I can't be your bi-curious experiment. It feels like I'm being used."

My mouth goes sour. "Oh my god, no. I don't want that. I didn't think ... I'm sorry. You're absolutely right."

He gives me a sad smile. "I wish I wasn't. I've just been burned one too many times by guys who told me they wanted more but didn't. I know you're asking the opposite, but you'll have to figure out your place on the Kinsey scale some other way."

I nod. "I don't want to ever make you feel bad. I'm not going to, um, use you. To figure out my sexuality, I mean."

"Thanks." Shelby lowers his voice. "Then we're lucky we have our relationship defined. It's to get you health insurance because you helped save me, and it's the least I could do to pay you back for getting hurt in the process."

"Shelby. You don't owe me anything."

"Okay, but in any case, you're straight."

"Straight-ish," I correct.

His jaw drops open, and it would be comical if my heart weren't pounding right now. "What?"

I shrug. "I'm not sure I *am* straight."

"Really?"

"Yeah."

We fall silent.

Why is my heart beating so fast? It must be the margarita. It must. The server interrupts us to tell us our meals will be out soon.

Shelby looks miserable. I want to kiss the frown off him, but that doesn't respect what he needs.

I squeeze his shoulder. "How about this? You're not my experiment without your express consent, every step of the way. Just know that if I were to do anything with a man, I think I'd do it with you." That statement makes all the butterflies in my stomach flutter.

"Thanks." He presses his lips together, then gives a little nod. "I still want to kiss you, though. I, uh, like it. I like being affectionate."

"Will that mess with your head?"

"I don't think so."

"Then we can kiss on your terms." If he needs space to figure out what's okay, I can give it to him.

He sets his shoulders. "I'm good with it. Kissing, I mean. Kiss me as much as you want."

I do—kiss him again, that is, though maybe not as much as I want, since while the restaurant isn't busy in the middle of the afternoon on a weekday, we are still in a public place—and it feels just as amazing as the other times.

Maybe labels don't matter. Maybe I can just concentrate on how this feels—he's aggressive but, at the same time receptive, and I'm really digging it. And I know we won't go any further.

Why do I feel disappointed?

"Anything else you want to do today?" I ask, when we break apart.

He swallows hard. "Nah. I think we've had enough excitement for one day. Noah only gave me half the day off, so I'll need to drop you at home, then go back to work. I can make you an appointment to get your ankle looked at. Do you have a regular doctor?"

I shake my head.

"Want to go to mine? Dr. Logan usually sets aside a block of time for urgent appointments."

"That would be great, yeah."

Our meals arrive, and we dig in.

* * *

At home, I take off my wedding suit and boutonniere, put on sweatpants and a T-shirt, and ice my ankle. Moving around so much today really did a number on me, so I settle on the couch to watch a marathon of *Going RV*. When Shelby comes back after work, he knocks on the glass door and comes in, then cringes yet again at the bare-bones conditions. I cringe, too, because he's right that the place is basically uninhabitable.

My heart does a happy little flip at the sight of his friendly face, and I turn the TV off. It's good to see him, even though we spent hours together this afternoon.

"I brought you dinner," he says, and joy bubbles up inside me.

"Wow. Thank you."

I like having Shelby around. While I grew up in a noisy house, I'd gotten used to the quiet of living on my own. But it was lonely.

He's not loud or obtrusive, but he is a presence. A kind one. Even in the short period of time he's been here, Shelby has done thoughtful things for me. On top of the big, obvious one, that is. Like, he walks in and starts washing the coffee mugs that were in the sink. Last night, along with bringing me dinner and crutches, he stocked up on a few food staples that I was out of.

He also isn't making me feel like an invalid, even though he's caring for me. After he finishes puttering around in the kitchen, he brings me a glass of ice water and some Aleve.

I'm not totally sure how I found this guy, but I like him.

Shelby's wearing black leggings with a tight T-shirt, and the close-fitting garments show off his body. I find myself looking at him. At the way his legs flex. The way his butt is kind of cute, actually. The way a sliver of his skin shows above the leggings and below the hem of his shirt. I also find myself wondering what he looks like without clothes.

Is that even okay, based on our rules?

I was raised to believe same-sex relationships are nothing out of the ordinary—both my siblings came out by the time they were fourteen, plus my parents have friends who are in same-sex couples, so we've always been accustomed to non-heteronormative relationships. But it's very weird for me to be perving on my ... husband.

Well, when I put it that way, it seems very *normal* to be perving on him. *Not* ogling my husband would be the odd thing, though I'm not going to disrespect him and make it obvious.

But I think I'm attracted to him. He's got a gorgeous smile, white teeth, and dark eyes that are so full of life.

He brings cartons of delicious-smelling Chinese food over to the coffee table, then fusses with plates, dishing up servings for both of us. When he pauses to survey his work, I tug him by the back of his waistband, which startles him into sitting on my lap. "What?" he yelps.

"Oh my god, did I get one of your bruises?" I start inspecting his arms for any painful spots I might have touched.

"No. You just surprised me."

"It's good to see you."

He gives me a hug. "Same." He's careful not to jostle my ankle, and he's light in my lap. He's making my cock wake up, despite the pain in my foot.

But he moves and sits next to me, and with the distraction of our dinner, all is forgotten. We chat about his day, and he tells me he made me a doctor's appointment for tomorrow, and something about that simple act loosens the stress that's been overtaking me.

I will get better.

For now, I pass him some egg rolls, and we eat them with way too much sweet-and-sour sauce, laughing because everything gets a bit sticky.

Once our plates are empty, we crack open our fortune cookies.

"What does yours say?" I ask.

Shelby holds up the little white slip. "You are kind, and people like you."

"While that's true, it's more of an affirmation cookie, not a fortune cookie."

He laughs. "I'm going to buy more of these. They tell me what I want to hear. What does yours say?"

"Be careful in matters of the heart." I frown. "That's an advice cookie. Not a fortune cookie."

"Ha. Well, maybe it's good advice." Shelby takes the two slips of paper and puts them on the table. He picks up our plates and cleans up, forbidding me to stand. Then he returns and curls next to me on the couch like a kitten. I wrap an arm around his shoulder and bury my face in his hair.

"Did you just sniff my hair?" he asks.

"Kinda, yeah. You always smell really good."

"I do, don't I?"

I chuckle. He reaches for the remote, moving away from me to do so, and I make this weird noise I don't think I've ever made before. Kind of a whine.

He looks over his shoulder at me in surprise. "You really don't want to be alone."

"No," I say, my voice husky.

"Okay, hubby." Tucking himself back into my side, he aims the remote at the television and turns it on.

"Want to watch *Building Off the Grid*?"

Shelby grins. "Absolutely. Does that show give you ideas for the house?"

My stomach sinks. "I wish."

I don't want him to know that I actually don't have great plans for this place. It was clear that the mold-ridden drywall, popcorn ceiling, and asbestos in the attic had to go. But now? I'm not sure what I'm going to do. Especially since I'm hurt and so low on cash.

So I don't elaborate. Thankfully, he doesn't ask any more questions. We simply watch television together until it gets late. Finally, after an episode with a particularly weird, unlivable home—they were planning on using a solar-powered outhouse in Alaska in winter, sheesh—he leans over and kisses me.

Shelby kisses *me*. It's the first time I've been kissed by a guy. And I like it.

"I should go to bed," he says. "Thanks for a wonderful wedding day."

"Yep," I say. "Same. I mean, thanks. For everything."

He gives me a wistful look. "Goodnight, Cam."

"Goodnight, husband," I say, and his eyebrows shoot up.

Before I can help myself, I tug him by his shirt, and he comes willingly to give me a hug. Then he stands and heads toward the door to the backyard. I can't help thinking that this isn't the way it's supposed to go.

"Is anything wrong?" I ask.

His cheeks redden. "I guess I never thought I'd be spending my wedding night by myself."

"Oh." *Oh.* I make a fast decision. "Give me a few, and I'll join you," I say. "If you don't mind," I hasten to add. "And we won't do anything. Just sleep. Maybe kiss, if you want. But if it will make you feel right, then we should do it."

He holds up his hand. "Don't worry about it."

"I don't want to be alone on my wedding night, either," I admit.

His gaze softens, and warmth rushes into my chest.

"I'll be there after I brush my teeth?" I ask.

Shelby swallows hard and nods, and my heart is in my throat. "Okay, see you then," he says.

A few minutes later, I'm stepping out into the night, swinging on my crutches. Frogs croak, and a car drives past on the street out front, but it's pretty quiet otherwise.

I knock gently on the guesthouse door, and in a moment, Shelby opens it. His hair is a mess like it never is during the day, his spun sugar hair going every which way. He's clearly washed his face and brushed his teeth, smelling minty again. Now that his makeup is gone, his bruising is more visible. I *really* wish I'd hurt Evan more.

"Um," I say, rubbing the back of my neck.

He opens his arms. "Come here."

I step forward, and he wraps his arms around my waist. He's shorter and much smaller than I am, but I like him holding me. It feels like I can shelter him but that he's keeping me up, too.

He takes my hand and pulls me toward the bed. After I settle my crutches to the side, within easy reach, I take off my shirt and strip down to my boxer briefs, then crawl into his bed, which is newer and better than mine. I'd intended it for future Airbnb guests, but I'm glad Shelby gets to use it now.

Shelby mutters something under his breath, then takes off his leggings and slides in next to me, wearing his T-shirt and briefs.

There's a moment where we both look up at the ceiling, and then I flop over and beckon to him. "C'mere," I say.

He grins and snuggles up next to me. I reach behind me to turn off the light.

Holding him in my arms, my head on his soft pillow, I watch as he drifts to sleep.

Shelby's platinum hair gleams in the moonlight, and his warm weight against my body feels right. I'm a little scared to move, not wanting to touch him more than I'm allowed. He's this combination of soft and hard—velvety skin, lean muscle. It's entrancing. But I keep my hands where they are and tug him closer to me.

I think about the day.

I'm *married*. To a *man*. *This* man.

It seems I really picked a good one, for not knowing him very well. With his scent relaxing me, as well as the security of knowing I'm going to get medical care, I drift off, too.

At some point in the middle of the night, I wake up, and Shelby's spread out on top of me, fast asleep. His nose turns up a little bit, and it's adorable. He has a slight, whiffling snore. My hand moves to play with his pale hair, his lean back. It even goes exploring to the round curve of his ass on one journey.

I've never experienced anything like this. It's not like being with a woman. The stick he's poking my leg with tells me that, as well as his flat, hard chest.

Also ... my husband is *gorgeous*.

With that thought, I go back to sleep.

CHAPTER 9

Shelby

I wake before my alarm, drifting to consciousness when I realize I'm being held by my husband.

To repeat: *my husband.*

And wow, we spent our wedding night in the same bed. I never would've figured that would happen under the circumstances. Not that I had that much chance to think before jumping into marriage —or bed—with Camden. His huge, defined bicep eclipses my arm, and he feels solid and amazing behind me.

There's also something solid and amazing pressing against my ass.

I need to pee, and brush my teeth and make myself more presentable. So I reluctantly wiggle out of his grasp and slip into the bathroom to freshen up. Once I'm done, I return to resume the same position, except Cam isn't wearing a shirt, and until he crawled into my bed last night, I'd never seen him shirtless. I have to take a moment to inspect him.

I sigh hard.

He's just so handsome. His morning stubble and messy hair make him look rumpled and vulnerable. And, much to my delight —okay, and some frustration—when he took off his shirt, I learned that both his nipples are pierced. I'm not saying I would've married him for that reason alone, but it is a bonus.

A bonus I can't enjoy to the fullest extent.

I watch his chest rise and fall for a moment before I slide back in next to him. When I do, he snuffles happily, and I smile into my pillow.

I really want to kiss him. I want to jump his bones, actually.

But I can resist. I'm going to respect my own boundaries. I have to.

My thoughts drift until he moves and blinks his eyes open.

"Hi," I say. My anxious brain worries that he's going to run away screaming once he realizes what he did yesterday.

"Hey. Morning." Cam leans over, and before I can go down any mental rabbit hole, he's kissing me.

Okay. Yes.

It's a quick peck, but I don't let him get away with that. I tug the back of his neck, and he grunts a little but moves between my legs, not protesting. And when I part my lips, he slides his tongue into my mouth.

This in turn wakes up my cock, which had been idling but now is revving to go. He's still hard, too, and his cock brushes against my leg.

We break apart for a moment, panting, and he blinks rapidly. "Sorry."

"Don't be," I say, breathless.

"No, Shelby," Cam says. "I listened to you yesterday. Let's just … not."

I will not roll my eyes. I will not sigh in exasperation. I will stay strong. I will be grateful he's doing what I asked. My mind will quit spinning off on tangents about what I'd like to do with my husband if things were different between us.

"Thanks," I force out, then berate myself. Because I could maybe have had some morning somethin'-somethin' with my handsome husband, but because of my *principles* and my *self-worth*, I'm going to deprive myself.

No nookie for me. Even if I want it.

Cam gives me a shy smile. "Okay." He clears his throat. "What time—" My phone alarm sounds, and we both groan. I fumble to turn it off, and Cam reluctantly lets me.

I sit up. "I'm sorry for the mixed messages. Obviously, I don't know what I want. Or rather, I know what I *should* want, which is different than what I *do* want."

"S'okay. No need to figure everything out this second. We can go at your pace. Or not at all."

"It doesn't matter right now, because we need to get ready," I say. "Or we'll be late to your doctor's appointment."

Cam grumbles, "I know." He gives me a little smile. "Sorry. I guess I just wanted to not have real life break in."

"How about you go take a quick shower, and I'll do the same, and then I'll make us breakfast and we can go to the doctor's office."

"Sounds like a plan." He smiles and kisses me, then gets off me gingerly. His dick is a solid pole in his boxers, and I want it so bad —in me, anywhere. Or at least to touch it and make him feel good.

But. I have rules.

No straight experiments. Or straight-ish experiments. (Anymore.)

He shrugs on his shirt and throws his sweats over his shoulder before using his crutches to get out of my bedroom. I watch his tight ass go and groan loudly again when the door closes behind him.

I take the fastest shower I can, then figure Cam needs help getting dressed. And yes, I'm both ignoring the fact that he's managed to dress himself the past few days *and* hoping to catch him partially dressed.

He's my husband. Sue me.

I round the corner to his bedroom, which is one of the very few rooms in his house that has drywall, and knock on the door. "Hey, Cam," I say. "Do you need any help?"

"Ugh. Maybe. Come in."

I do, and holy shit, he's standing there wearing only a sage green towel.

Everything that was on display in my bed is here waiting for me, again. His muscular chest. His trim waist, and that tidy happy trail down from his belly button. A bulge in the front of his towel. Those damned barbells in his nipples.

I want him.

But then I notice how swollen Cam's ankle looks, and I remember what we're actually doing. He tries to hobble to his dresser, and I dart into the room. "No," I say, pushing gently on his chest.

He's *muscular*. I suppress a whimper.

"Let me get it. What do you want to wear?" I open the first drawer and luck out, since it's full of folded socks and underwear.

"Um, those," he says, pointing to a pair of white boxer briefs.

I hold them out for him so he can step into first one leg hole and then the other, and then I slide the briefs up his hairy thighs. He smells like body wash and aftershave and deodorant, and oh god, he's mouthwatering.

It's not lost on me that if I bent down just a little more and moved his towel, I could get his dick in my mouth, and he groans. "Don't look at me like that, Shelby."

"I don't mean to tease. I did want to see you, because you're handsome as hell, but I genuinely wanted to help you get dressed."

"To be fair," Cam says, "helping someone put clothes *on* is not usually any kind of foreplay."

Foreplay.

I want foreplay with my husband.

"You have a point," I whisper.

"We're going to respect your wishes and go slow." He grins. "I can take care of myself in the shower just fine."

Now *that's* an image. I'm *so* questioning my previous resolve.

But I'm also questioning the premise. Cam may be new at letting himself be touched by a man, but he's doing a great job of it. And if he's my husband, maybe it's not the same thing as guys before. With Evan, I thought I was escaping from Tyler. John-John. Alex. Frankie. Any of the other "straight" guys I've been with and who dumped me when I wanted more than they could publicly give me. Of course, Evan turned out to have his own issues.

Cam's not hiding, and he's not hiding *me*.

So maybe doing things with him is consistent with my new determination to not mess with straight guys after all, since he's certainly not seemed ashamed of me the few times I've been in public with him.

Or maybe I've just hung out with enough lawyers to be able to make a persuasive argument for whatever I want.

Right now, it doesn't matter, since we have to get going. I'll give him the benefit of the doubt and see how he acts with me today.

I turn around to give him privacy to pull his underwear up the rest of the way, and I start opening drawers. "Okay, what else do you want to wear?"

"Um, T-shirt and jeans, I think. Or maybe sweats."

I nod and hand him a navy blue T-shirt, and he puts it on. Then I get out some dark gray sweatpants and help him with those. I try not to linger on his shapely legs or the bulge in his boxer briefs.

Soon he's dressed, except his feet are bare and his hair is wet. And I still want him.

"Let me get your boot," I say, gesturing to where he'd left it by the bed.

He starts to hop without his crutches. "I can do it."

"I know. But I kind of like helping you."

"Okay," he says. "I appreciate that."

Somehow his acquiescence is so damn hot. Because Cam is used to being able to do anything. It's not in his nature to accept help—and I think doing so makes him a bigger person.

I should take notes.

Now that I think about it, Cam has listened to me all along. Even in those first moments with Evan, he was willing to back off once he'd stood up for me. He listened when I suggested this out-there insurance solution. He listens to me chatter about work and everything else.

Sigh. He's getting under all my defenses, and it's making me uncomfortable—uncomfortable with how happy I am when I'm around him, that is.

We get Cam's ankle set up, and he slides his other foot into a flip-flop, then uses crutches to go out to the kitchen, such as it is. I make us pancakes on his electric griddle and brew coffee, and he sniffs appreciatively. "Thanks," he says. "Living by myself, I forget to eat properly sometimes."

"No worries. Pancakes are easy."

"But I feel like things are unbalanced between us. Let me do the dishes, at least."

I cluck my tongue in disapproval. "Nope. There's plenty of time for you to do that once your foot is feeling better."

"I still feel like I need to do more."

"What you need to do is heal."

Cam sighs. "Yeah, okay." We eat our breakfast, and I tidy up. Then he hobbles over to get his keys, wallet, and phone.

"Do you want me to drive you?" I'm dressed for work, where I'll be headed later, but I've called in to use sick time for kin care this morning. The first time I've ever done that.

"I can do it," he says.

"I know you can. But let me help?" I peer up at him.

Cam locks his eyes on me, then clears his throat. "Okay, fine. Yeah. I could use a hand. Let's take my car so at least you're not out the gas."

He doesn't sound begrudging, although I can tell he's not happy about asking for more help. I understand how he feels. I want to be able to do everything on my own, but it just doesn't work out that way sometimes.

We get into his big truck, and I have to scoot the seat up so I can reach the gas pedal. I feel like I'm approximately ten years old. Not that ten-year-olds drive trucks. But with my feet swinging, I just feel young.

Cam doesn't say a word. Most people I know would at least smile at my being so short, but he doesn't.

Maybe he didn't notice. Maybe he's in too much pain. Or, more likely, maybe he's simply too nice to say something mean like that.

"This thing is huge," I say.

"That's what he said," Cam replies.

I grin and start the truck, then back slowly out of the driveway, wondering how I'm going to maneuver this thing through LA traffic.

I needn't have worried. Everyone gets out of my way. Apparently that's the secret benefit to having a Truckasaurus—everyone bows down before you.

When we get to Dr. Logan's office, it occurs to me that Cam may want privacy for a doctor's visit. But just then he smiles at me and asks, "Do you mind coming inside with me?"

"Not at all." I'm familiar with the staff, since this is my long-time regular doctor, and I know there are good magazines in the waiting room. Today, one of the *Star Wars* movies is playing on a wall-mounted screen, two Jedi battling it out with their lightsabers.

Camden fills out new-patient papers, and then, when nurse

Marlena calls him, he tilts his head. "Can my husband come with me?"

Holy macaroni, Cam called me his husband to a stranger again—well, a stranger to him.

But maybe it's for verisimilitude. After all, if the insurance company wanted to make a stink about his coverage, they might ask the staff here how we act together. Do they ever do that? Perhaps.

Marlena does a double take. "I didn't know you got married, Shelby! Congratulations!"

"Yeah, we're newlyweds," I say.

"That's awesome!" She nods. "Shelby is welcome to join you."

I hop up from my chair and follow him down the hall to the small exam room.

Cam sits on the crinkly paper of the exam table while the nurse takes his vitals, and I claim a visitor's chair.

He swallows, and I watch his Adam's apple bob. After she leaves, he says, "Thanks for coming. I don't actually like going to the doctor."

"Do you think you're going to need surgery?"

"That's one of the options they mentioned at urgent care. I guess we'll find out." He sighs. "I'm glad you're here."

"There's no place else I'd rather be." I don't know Cam very well, but dammit, I'm going to support him and be an actual husband for however long we're together. After that, well, maybe we can still be friends. But I want him to know that his health and well-being matter to me.

Before I can stop myself, I reach over and squeeze his hand, and he squeezes mine back. I don't know why something as simple as holding Cam's hand makes me so warm inside. Maybe because it feels like a connection to him, and that might be what I've been trying to get my entire life. Connection to a special someone.

We keep holding hands until Dr. Logan comes into the room.

Even then, we don't break apart until we have to—when the doctor makes Cam lie back so he can examine his leg.

Dr. Logan looks at the X-rays the urgent care sent over, a tech takes a few more, and they do other tests. Eventually, Dr. Logan confirms that Cam has two hairline fractures in some part of his foot—don't ask me what the bones are. Cam can either have surgery, although they're concerned about the screw splintering his bone, or he can keep zero weight on his foot for twelve weeks. There's a "bone stim" procedure he can have that will stimulate the healing process. He's going to need a series of casts and braces, some expensive carbon fiber insoles for special shoes he'll have to wear, plus lots of physical therapy that will continue even after he's medically cleared to put weight on it.

I can tell Cam thinks twelve weeks is a long time, but my stomach sinks. We probably will be divorced by the new year.

Still, it's quite a bit of care Cam will need. The knowledge that we've gone through all this rigmarole for a worthwhile purpose settles me. We've done the right thing.

Cam decides to go with the no-surgery option, they put a cast on his ankle, and he receives a prescription for pain relief along with a bunch of other instructions, which Dr. Logan tells to me as much as to Cam. I'm happy to think that I'll be able to help take care of my husband.

On the way home, we stop to fill his prescription, which he takes right away.

As we drive back to his house, I'm amused at how quickly the painkiller loosens him up. To be fair, there's quite a bit of traffic today, so everything is taking longer than it should, and breakfast was a couple of hours ago, so the medication is probably hitting hard.

"You know what I was thinking?" Cam says. His voice is a tad slurred, and it's adorable.

"What's that?" I ask, hiding my smile. I'm also glad that I drove.

"Have you ever seen *Star Wars*?"

"Yes."

"All the *Star Wars*. I mean more than one war of the *Star Wars*. More than one *movie*."

"Yes, I think I've seen most of them," I say. And OMG he's so cute when he's loopy.

"Have you ever noticed how there's no galactic OSHA?"

I snort. "What?"

"I mean, what the hell? There's all these bridges without railings where if you fall, you fall into infinite space. The least they could do is put up a barrier. If I have to wear a hard hat when I'm on a job site with scaffolding, you'd think that they could protect the Death Star. Someone needs to do an IIPP or whatever it's called. Injury and illness prevention plan."

"I think you're on to something. I'll see if my office can prepare a galactic OSHA IIPP," I say, giggling.

He nods, satisfied, then rests his head against the window.

When we get to his place, I walk him inside and settle him on the couch. He kisses me before I leave, and it's long and deep enough that my toes curl and I have to sternly remind myself I'm supposed to be going to work, not throwing my resolutions to the wind and dragging his drugged but very appealing butt into the bedroom. He also gives me a goofy smile, which makes me happier than it should.

I switch to my car and drive to my office, arriving a good four hours late. But the first thing I see when I walk in is a large vase of flowers and silver and white balloons at the reception desk reading "Mr. and Mr." Everyone comes out of their offices, clapping and congratulating me.

My eyes tear up. I love the people I work with.

"Happy wedding!" Alden says.

"Thanks!"

Charlie smirks at me, and Reyna gives me a speculative smile. She also gives me a hug.

Noah hugs me, too. "I think I've figured out why you did this," he whispers. "And it's pretty generous of you."

I shrug. "It's the right thing to do."

I'm suddenly hit by panic that someone is going to call us out for insurance fraud. Except ... we're *really* married. And we can stay married as long as we want. So I grin and accept the surprised well-wishes from everyone. "Congratulations!" Sam says, and I get another hug.

People slowly head back to work, and I'm left with a small group surrounding me and asking questions like "How long have you known Camden?" For years, actually. And "When did you know he was the one?" Very recently.

Although, truth be told, I've had a crush on him since I first saw him at a firm party when we hired Charlie and Reyna a few years ago.

Danny cuffs my bicep. "What's it like being an old married man?" he asks.

I laugh. "I've been married for approximately twenty-four hours, which is also my age. That's barely old or married."

Danny grins. "Okay, fair enough. But you're good?"

I think of what it felt like to have lunch with Cam. How it felt to sleep next to him. His kisses this morning. What his almost-naked body looks like. How much I want to eat him up. His goofy *Star Wars* thoughts.

No. I'm thinking how glad I am that he's getting medical care. That's it.

"I'm so good," I say, and I mean it.

CHAPTER 10

Camden

I spend most of the afternoon floating, thanks to the pain meds, and eventually end up napping. When I wake up, it's after five, and not only is my husband standing before me— my sister is, too. I blink and sit up, rubbing my eyes.

"Oh my god, Camden, you have to tell Mom and Dad at dinner tonight," Reyna says, reaching down and pushing my shoulder.

I yawn. "Tell them what?"

She puts both hands on her hips and glares. "That you're married. And to a man. Shelby walked into work yesterday with a ring, and Charlie fessed up. Plus, we had a little party for Shelbs this afternoon." She gives Shelby a small smile.

"You don't think they'll care about my ankle? I'm hurt." I hold back a grin. "Literally."

Reyna groans. "They're going to be upset about that, too. *Obviously*. But you've broken bones before. You know they're going to be concerned about you, with a wedding and all. After what happened last year ..."

Her words send ice through my veins, but it's not like I intentionally kept something from Shelby. To be fair, I barely had any conversations with him before marrying him.

Shelby scrutinizes my face. "Is there something I'm missing?"

My cheeks burn. "Yeah. I got left at the altar." I affect my best blasé tone to keep the hard shell that protects me in place.

It's never easy reliving that day, and seeing Shelby jerk his head back with an incredulous stare and a gasp doesn't help. He swats my arm. "You're joking." He looks to Reyna for confirmation.

She shakes her head. "It was bad."

"I thought I'd heard something about you and an engagement, but then it went away," Shelby whispers. "I didn't really think about what had happened. I'm so sorry."

I cross my arms. "Not your fault." Then I relent, because he deserves to know, but my voice is strained and my pulse is racing. "I worked for Leah's parents' construction company starting when I was eighteen. She worked in the office. I used to have coffee with her in the mornings, which turned to her bringing me lunch on sites. Which turned to me asking her out to dinner. And so on."

Shelby nods. "Okay."

"After a few years, I thought I was in love with her." I clear my throat, but it doesn't relieve the pain in my chest. Still, I soldier on. "Anyway, she said yes when I proposed. We planned our wedding, sent invitations, booked the place and the caterers, the whole nine yards." I sound bitter. Probably because I am. "The day of the wedding came, and everything was normal. I'm in a tuxedo, standing at the front of the church. All our family and friends in attendance. She's in a beautiful white dress, and music plays. But I could tell something was off by the way she wouldn't look at me when she was coming down the aisle. The ceremony starts. I say my vows to her. And she says, in answer to the question, 'Do you take this man, Camden, to be your wedded husband ...?'"—my voice cracks—"'No.'"

Heat licks through my body as I remember how heartbroken

and mortified I was. It felt like I'd been hit by a truck, burned on a pyre, and pissed on, all at the same time.

A chain wrapped around my chest that day, locking my feelings up tight.

Shelby's hands fly to his face. "Oh my god. Camden. I'm so sorry that happened."

"Me fucking too, Shelby," I say bitterly. "Me fucking too. Although in hindsight, I likely dodged a bullet, even though it would be nice if it hadn't happened *at* the wedding." The wedding I insisted on paying for—photographer, invitations, tuxedo rentals, everything. Her parents were going to pay for the honeymoon. They'd bought trip insurance and got a refund. I didn't have insurance.

Seems to be a trend.

So between that and buying this house ... I have nothing saved anymore. Reyna looks sympathetic but thankfully doesn't say anything.

"What happened after that?" Shelby asks.

"Leah turned and ran out of the church, leaving me standing there with a few hundred people staring at me. It was awkward." My chest aches as I remember how devastating it was to be rejected like that.

"He stormed out and got drunk with Charlie and me," Reyna says.

I glare at her. "Thanks, I can tell it. But yes, I left and found the nearest bar. Oh, and when she dumped me, her dad felt uncomfortable having me around, so I lost my job, too, which is how I ended up without health insurance. It just hasn't been at the top of the priority list while I was getting my own business started."

"That sucks," Shelby says. "I'm so sorry," he repeats.

"To make matters worse, now she's getting married to someone else and keeps trying to invite me to her wedding like she needs to atone or wants closure." I roll my eyes. "Nothing's incomplete. She didn't love me. End of story." I sigh and look at Shelby. "So, yeah. I was supposed to be married before."

Even if this is only a temporary thing, I don't want Shelby to feel like he's *less than*. I wrap my arm around his waist and tug him next to me on the couch. "I think Reyna's right. We need to tell my parents." I put my fingertips on his chin and gently turn his head toward me so I can study his face. "I can show you off."

The panic in his eyes would be comical if I didn't feel the same thing.

"Hey, babe," I say. Reyna's watching me cuddle Shelby like she's a bird of prey, but I don't miss the way her eyes go soft at the endearment. Whatever. She can think what she wants. "You don't have to come with me. But it would be weird if they didn't meet you."

"Are they going to be pissed that we essentially eloped?" Shelby asks.

I rub my face. "Yeah, probably. They'll want to throw us some kind of celebration or reception, even if it's just a barbecue in their backyard."

"They don't need to go to that trouble. We can tell them it's only for insurance."

"Ugh." I sigh. "I don't want to see the look on my mom's face if we say that. She's a hopeless romantic and has been stymied since none of her kids have married yet. She was so excited about my and Leah's wedding."

"Well, I mean." He throws out his hands. "I'm available to do whatever you'd like me to do."

"Yeah," I say quietly. "You have been available for me, and I appreciate it."

"It's my pleasure."

"Then ... want to come to dinner with me and my family tonight?"

"I'll be there with explanations on." Shelby grins. I hug him again and kiss his temple.

Reyna eyes me speculatively, but I don't care. I like Shelby, and he's my husband. While we're together, I'll cuddle him if I want to.

"Where's dinner going to be?" I ask her. "Mom and Dad's, or what?"

"No, the trendy place across from the Santa Monica Pier. I forgot the name. I'll text it to you. I'll confirm with her that you two are coming. The reservation isn't until seven thirty, so you have time before you have to be there."

I stretch and rub the back of my neck, then look at Shelby. "You good with hanging out with the whole Cooper clan?"

"I wouldn't miss it."

* * *

Since the prescription painkillers made me a little too loose, I'm opening drawers in the bathroom, looking for the over-the-counter pain reliever. I'm sure I used it last, but maybe Shelby took the bottle for some reason? I hobble over to ask him, because my ankle is really starting to ache.

It's a windy, warm day, the sun bright, and the pool is sparkling clean. I'm dying to go for a swim once the cast is off. I'll just have to be patient.

When I make it to Shelby's door, I hold up my hand to knock, but the breeze blows it open. I guess he hadn't fully closed it.

I stiffen. Shelby is bent over, sliding some tight jeans up his lean legs, his little ass facing me.

An ass that's toned and covered with black briefs in some formfitting, futuristic fabric—German engineered or something.

His skin looks so soft. He's naturally a deep, dark tan, and he's, well. Hmm.

Sexy.

I'm not sure what to think about that, but I realize I've been standing here too long without saying something, so I clear my throat. He startles and turns around quickly. His platinum hair is standing up straight, and it's a little staticky in this dry air. I want to play with it.

I clear my throat again. "Um, I was looking for the Aleve."

Shelby frowns. "It's in the cabinet in the bathroom in the main house."

Shaking my head, I say, "I looked. I didn't see it."

He reaches for a T-shirt and shrugs it over his head, the movement drawing my attention to his torso. He may be much, much smaller than me, but he's very defined. His brown nipples pebble, and he finishes pulling up his jeans, shoving his ass in there the final amount.

I'm bummed to lose the view.

"I'm sorry to make you look for it," he says softly.

God, what is his voice doing to me? It's not just the pitch—low and soothing—but it's, again, sexy. No wonder his job is answering phones. He's got a great phone voice.

I wonder if he could be a phone sex operator—and, nope, not going there.

Not going to think about what kind of fantasies Shelby could spin for a caller.

Not going to think about what his skin feels like.

I already know I like kissing him. And sleeping with him.

And I'm not doing anything more, because we aren't really a couple and we've agreed we aren't going to do that.

I limp behind him back to the main house and to the bathroom, and he reaches up on tiptoes and finds the bottle, which was *right there*. Of course. "Ugh. Thanks. I guess I wasn't looking for that color or something. I just missed it."

"It's okay. It happens."

We're both standing in a small space, and I realize I'm keeping him from the door. I back away, but he still has to brush against me to get through, and I hold my breath.

"Are you okay to go to dinner?" he asks, voice laced with concern. "You're not in too much pain?"

"It hurts," I admit.

He tuts. "Then let me get you some water. Hang on."

I make my way to the couch, although I think he might have meant I should stay in the bathroom.

By the time I'm seated, Shelby is standing there with a glass of water. He takes the medicine bottle from me and shakes out the dose, then hands it to me like I'm a child.

"Thanks," I mutter.

He leans toward me, a knee on the couch, and puts the back of his hand on my forehead. "You seem on edge. Are you having second thoughts about me meeting your parents?"

"No, not at all." I'm irritated, but it's not because of my injury. It's because he's so near. It's because he's scrambling my circuits. It's because I can't think when he's around.

It's because I want to kiss him again. I go to stand up, but he takes both hands and presses down on my shoulders. "Just sit for a minute and let the medicine start to work. We still have enough time to get to the restaurant."

Then I notice how we're positioned. He's practically straddling me. And my dick is starting to pay attention. Everything I thought I knew about myself seems to go out the window when Shelby's around.

I could take the chance. I could pull him down and kiss him. I think he'd come willingly, because he seems to like being kissed.

But I'm not sure that's the right thing for us to do.

He goes to stand up, and, well, fuck it.

I reach out and grab him, holding him securely to me, and he gets my intent. I reach up as he leans down, and our lips meet. In doing so, his thigh brushes my dick, and I shudder.

Shelby gives me a quizzical look. And before he can say anything, I'm pillaging his mouth.

He opens for me, letting me explore. But he's not passive at all. He gives as good as he gets, and he gets quite a bit.

My dick is getting harder, and now I can feel his. He's lightly grinding against my thigh, almost unconsciously. Not enough to rub the zipper against his dick so it hurts. Just ... aiming for a little relief.

Then he jerks back, holding his hands up. "I'm sorry."

I blink. "Don't be. I want it. You're really fucking hot."

"God," he groans. "You drive me up the wall, Camden Cooper." And his mouth is on mine again.

Only this time, he's in charge of the kiss. I battle back, but he takes over, and fuck. There's something hot about him being the aggressor. I'm not used to that.

But I could get used to it. Very easily.

I cup his ass, and he grinds into me, and I shift so I'm lying on the couch the long way and he's straddling me for real. He snakes a hand under my shirt and tweaks one of my nipples, tugging on the piercing, which makes me gasp. I can't seem to get enough of kissing him. He's the right size. He fits in my hands. I like the way he feels, and I love the way he tastes. I just want to be with him.

I'm also aware that I'm painfully turned on.

"Pretty damned sure I'm not so straight," I mutter.

"Oh, god," he whispers.

We break apart. "I think we need to go to dinner," I say.

"Nooooo," he whines.

"I know." I grimace. "I don't want to see them, either."

"It's not that." He gestures between us. "I want ..." He sighs and looks at his watch. "Never mind. We need to leave, or we'll be late."

With one more kiss, we pick ourselves up and go.

CHAPTER 11

Camden

When Shelby and I walk into the main dining room of the restaurant—well, Shelby walks; I swing my body on crutches—my mom stands up at the table and gasps.

"Camden Edward Cooper! What happened to you?"

I sit down next to her and stash the crutches. "I got married."

Her double take is comical. "What?" she shrieks, loud enough that the whole restaurant turns to look at her.

"Mom, meet Shelby Borchard." I pause. "My husband."

Mom looks back and forth between us, wondering if I'm pulling her leg.

Shelby holds out his hand to shake. She stares at it, then glances over at mine, seeing our rings. Then she pulls him in tight for a hug. "Your ... husband? I'm so confused." She blinks a few times and holds Shelby out to look at him. "I'm so glad to meet you, Shelby. I had no idea Camden was dating anyone."

"Or bisexual," Charlie pipes up.

Reyna shoves him.

Sitting on the far side of my brother, my dad also looks confused. "Well, congratulations to the newlyweds," he finally says, heartily. He gets up to shake Shelby's hand. "Welcome to the Cooper family."

They order champagne for the table, which I shouldn't have because of the pain relievers, but I have a sip anyway.

"I must say," Mom says, after we settle in and order food, "I wasn't expecting you to be *married*. Or even have a significant other. I wanted to know about *this*." She gestures at the boot on my foot and the crutches.

"I hurt my foot on a job," I say. It's somewhere close to true. Next door to true?

"Oh, honey. I'm so sorry."

"He was a real hero," Shelby says. "I saw him."

Dad smiles. "A chip off the old block, eh?"

I shrug. I mean, yeah. My father always has been my hero. He always did step in to fix things when they were wrong.

"When you get better," Charlie says, "we'll have to figure out the next project we'll do for Ad/VICE."

"Okay," I say. "Maybe we can get going on the interior of the house."

"Can I second that?" Shelby asks.

"What's wrong with it?" Mom asks. She hasn't been over in a while.

"I tore it down to the studs in a lot of places. I need to put up drywall and redo things."

"So he's staying in the pool house with me," Shelby says, which, again, is somewhere close to true.

"That's sweet," Mom says. "Shelby, what have your parents said about your marriage?"

He stiffens and turns red. "Um, I'm not very close to my family, so I haven't told them yet."

Mom looks sympathetic. "Well, then you can be a part of ours." And she skillfully changes the topic of conversation to Reyna's latest case.

I wonder what Shelby's relationship with his family is really like—and what his past boyfriends have been like. And whether I'll ever know him well enough for him to open up about any of that.

We manage to make it through dinner without too much more fuss, and an hour later, I talk Shelby into walking across the street to the Santa Monica Pier.

"But your crutches," he protests.

"I'm fine. We can sit on a park bench and eat an ice pop. I need to thank you for making it through a meal with my family."

"I thought they were pretty great," he says.

"Then, dessert?"

He nods, and we walk across the street.

When we come up to the ice cream stand, I order a lemon pop, and the server asks, "Does your friend want something, too?"

"Actually, he's my husband," I say, and Shelby smiles. I tug him to me, and he comes willingly, wrapping his arm around my waist. I nuzzle the top of his head.

She doesn't bat an eye. When Shelby says he'll have the same as me, she hands another lemon pop to him. I pay, and he holds both pops as we make our way over to an area with more booths and rides, where we find a bench to sit on and enjoy our goodies before they melt.

"Gotta get used to that," he says.

"Being called my husband?"

He grins. "Well, that, too. But I was thinking, having someone buy me a popsicle. And, you know, claim me."

"I'll fucking claim you," I say. "I always had to share things as a kid. I like having something—someone—that's just for me, even if it's only for a while."

He smiles. "I like that. I'll claim you back."

I want to kiss him for that, but we're both too sticky from the treats.

"What do you want to do next?" I gesture at the Ferris wheel. "Want to go up?"

Shelby blinks at me. He's sucking on the popsicle, and it looks kind of phallic.

It startles me that my husband is so fucking attractive. That's a weird statement, since you're supposed to be attracted to your spouse. Even in this marriage-of-convenience situation, though, I'm getting more and more attracted to him the more time I spend with him. Go figure.

"Sure," he says. "My treat."

While I want to argue with him, I can see the resolve in his eyes, so I relent. I'll get something else for him. "Sounds good."

We finish our popsicles, then Shelby buys two tickets for the Ferris wheel and we get in line.

The giant wheel stops, and a group of people get off. When it's our turn to get in and the operator is holding the door open for us, Shelby and I look at each other.

"Which seat do you want?" I ask, gesturing.

"Can we sit side by side? I don't want to sit alone. I'm nervous enough about heights."

"Of course," I say.

"Will we be fine with the weight if we sit on the same side?" he asks the operator.

"Yep." The guy smacks his gum and takes my crutches.

"Cool," Shelby says faintly, and I climb in after him.

The door is closed and secured behind us, and the Ferris wheel takes off.

"Whoa," he says. "Is this gonna ... This is gonna get high, isn't it?"

"Haven't you been on one of these before?" I ask.

"I don't remember." He looks a little sick.

"Come here," I say, holding my arm out to pull him to me. "You can close your eyes if you want."

The wheel lurches to a stop as they let more people on and off, and he takes the opportunity to scoot closer. The wind tousles our hair, and we're getting a better view of the attractions around us.

When we get up to the top, I bet we'll have a fantastic view of the ocean and the city.

Even though I know these things are safe—or at least sort of safe—my heart is still pounding, accelerating every time we stop and start. I'm good with roofs. Ferris wheels? They're less reliable. It's worse when we're up at the top, but I don't want Shelby to see me being tentative, because he's already scared. Looking at him gives me some resolve.

"I don't think I like this," he says. "We're just so high up. And out here in the air."

"Want to get off?" I ask. "I can yell at the operator."

"No, it's okay. I guess I just need to hang on. Grin and bear it."

"Lie back and think of England?" I ask.

He giggles. "Where did you get that?"

"My British grandmother said it once, and it made me laugh."

We jolt into motion again, and he clasps my thigh. "If this would be steadier, I'd do better," he says. "It's the starts and stops and the hanging out in the middle of nowhere, swinging, that's getting to me."

He needs a distraction. I can tell he's getting scared, and we still have to go through a bunch of stops before the wheel will go around a few times.

I make a quick decision. "Hey," I say, lowering my voice.

He looks up at me, and I kiss him. I know it's a high school move, kissing him on a Ferris wheel, where there's this heightened sense of danger, but I don't care. I want to kiss him, and I'll take the excuse. I concentrate on how much I like making out with him.

Because we're *making out*. He tastes like lemon, and his tongue is still cold from the ice pop, as is mine. His hands are cold, too, but he wraps them around me, and we just kiss. Our tongues enter each other's mouths, and the world starts to drop away.

Or maybe that's our stomachs dropping.

Or maybe it's my heart beating faster, because it's not only the ride but also the kiss.

I like kissing my husband. I like how handsome he is. I like his bleached hair and his gentle, mischievous eyes. And how he takes care of me. How generous he is. How he makes me feel seen and not just one in a crowd. He scoots closer to me, and the bucket we're in swings, and we both freeze.

"Shit," I say. "I don't want to scare you."

"You aren't scaring me. I wanted to be closer, but maybe that's a bad idea."

"I was trying to distract you. Was it working?"

His face falls. "Yeah."

"Hey. What's that face for?"

"It felt real."

"It was very real," I assure him. "You're very sexy."

"And you're very … formerly straight."

I shrug. "It's not like I have a problem with being gay. I just didn't think I was."

"Do you think you are now?"

I shake my head. "I might be bisexual. Or pansexual? I haven't figured out a label. Before, I noticed that guys were handsome or whatever, but I was never into the things Charlie was, so I figured I was straight. But," I shrug. "Maybe I was wrong."

To my surprise, Shelby pulls back and puts a hand on his hip. "Don't you do that now, Camden Cooper."

"Do what?"

"Be even more attractive. You're supposed to be unavailable."

I grin and lean over, pausing. When he nods, I kiss him. "No pressure. But I'm available to you."

He whines. "You're making it really hard to stick to my principles." His voice lowers, and I almost don't catch his muttered, "Or really hard in general." He sighs. "I know I'm the king of mixed messages, but I think I may want to stick to making out, nothing more. Until I get my head on right."

"You don't owe me or anyone any part of you."

"Thanks."

Shelby sits back, and I realize that the wheel hasn't stopped in a while. We get this whooshing, dropping, whooshing sensation over and over again as we go around and around, and I feel like I'm falling.

But I'm pretty sure it's not from the ride.

CHAPTER 12

Shelby

Okay, just because Cam is not so straight, and maybe likes me. And, okay, is married to me.

That *still* doesn't mean I should get my hopes up.

There's absolutely no reason why this relationship is anything other than me helping him for helping me. If he happens to figure out his sexuality in the mix, it's no big deal for either of us. Right?

But sex without emotion isn't what I want anymore. I've been fine with hookups in the past—mostly fine—but I've always secretly wanted the real thing.

The sun sets on the western horizon over the Pacific Ocean, and the lights of Los Angeles turn on behind us. Summer is ending. The days are getting shorter, and the nights are longer. The air smells like popcorn and cotton candy, and piped-in carousel noise is all around us.

As we go around on the Ferris wheel, I snuggle under Cam's outstretched arm. I'm reeling from our kisses, and my stomach is fluttering. When we dangle in midair while they load up another car, Cam must read the nervousness on my face, so he asks, "Tell me what it was like for you, growing up." He says it conversationally, as if he doesn't know what a big hole he just stepped in.

To be fair, he likely has zero idea that he stepped into a hole. But he did.

"It sucked," I say.

He barks out a laugh. "I'm sorry. I didn't mean to pry. You're just so much fun, I figured you had a fun childhood."

I shake my head. "I did *not* have a fun childhood. I had to make my own fun. So I imagined what life was going to be like when I got bigger." I huff. "I didn't get that much bigger."

Cam reaches over and squeezes my knee.

Do that a little higher, sweetheart.

But of course I don't say that, because Cam and I aren't like that. My resolve is slipping, like I'm trying to grab a wet water balloon but it's too hard to hold on to. Heh. Very hard.

"You don't have to talk about it," he assures me. "I wanted to know more about you, because I like you. But I don't mean to pry."

"It's fine," I say hastily. "I know. You weren't prying, and with a lot of people, it's not a tough question. But for those of us that it is a tough question, it's a *really* tough one." I scrub my face with my palms. "I wasn't abused. I think I was neglected a bit. My mom would tell me she wished I hadn't been born."

I didn't mean for that to slip out, but I can't seem to keep things from Cam. He feels so safe, like my little hiding place where I can go and won't get hurt.

His eyes narrow. "Shelby, that's abuse."

"No, she wasn't abusive. She never hit me, and I always had enough food and a place to stay and all that. Until I was eighteen. When I turned eighteen, she kicked me out. Said I was an adult now, and her job was done."

This is why I never celebrate my birthday, and why I keep the card she gave me to remind me not to expect people to go above and beyond what they are required to do.

"It sounds like emotional abuse, and she sounds horrible," Cam says. "I'm sorry to say that, but she does." The wheel swoops around one more time. I'm sure it's about time for us to be done. I'm certainly ready to get off this ride.

My shoulders slump. "When I was little, I thought it was normal. Then I grew older and looked around and saw that this wasn't happening to anyone else, and I started to think that it wasn't normal at all. That *I* wasn't normal."

"You're perfect. It's your mom who was wrong. She didn't treat you the way parents are supposed to treat their kids—with love."

"She resented me because she was so young when she got pregnant with me, and she felt like I ruined her life. She didn't get to go out and party, because she had a kid. She never had fun, because she had a kid."

"That's a poor excuse. I think kids can be fun—"

"Spoken like someone who doesn't have one."

"True. Still, there are plenty of people who have unplanned children but don't emotionally abuse their kids." He leans closer. "I think you may have some trauma, Shelby. I'm not a shrink or anything, but that had to have affected you."

I shrug so I don't cry.

Our basket finally makes its way down to the bottom, and we exit. Once Cam gathers his crutches, we make our way off, but then he tugs on my sleeve and pulls me into a space between two stores.

"Hey," he says, and he scoots closer. "Do you need a hug?"

I really, really do. I nod, still trying not to cry. He opens up his arms, and I fold myself into him. I've kissed my husband and slept next to him, but I may like his hugs the best. I rest my head against his chest and curl into him.

I have never felt more safe and comfortable—or more out of sorts—than I do right now. Cam is big and warm and solid. He smells like his body wash and deodorant: masculine, clean, strong. His heart thumps against my ear, and I can hear the rushing of my own blood, my harsher breathing, but also his steady breaths and his murmurs as he tells me it's all going to be okay.

If he wants me to feel better, big picture, he needs to not be so soothing, because I'm too conflicted right now. It seems like he's learning some new things about his sexuality, and hugging me has nothing to do with sex, anyway. But I confuse intimacy and affection and sex. They can be related, but they can also not be. "I don't know what I'm doing with you," I admit.

Cam strokes my hair. "What's going on with you? Inside that head, it seems like it's a tangled place."

"Yeah, it is. I always overanalyze everything. Or rather, I declare that I'm going to do something—or not do it—and then spend all my time talking myself into doing exactly the opposite. It's like I'm my own debate team."

He kisses the top of my head, and I sigh. I'm afraid I'm too loud, too needy. That I'm just too much.

But he cuddles me closer. "Hey," he says. "You can tell me anything. I'm not going to judge you."

"Why? Because you're my husband?"

Cam chuckles. "Yeah, I suppose. But no, it's because I like you. You want to be loved. I want to be the one who can at least tell you that it's okay to be you and that you are lovable just the way you are."

Now he's making it worse. Because I do want someone to love me, and I could see myself falling for Cam easily. But that's not our deal. On top of that, it feels wrong to think about looking at any other guy when I have Cam with me—not that I want to look at other guys. I have a sense of loyalty to him that's come on very strong from the moment we said our vows.

And that's probably something to analyze. Because I'm still loyal to my mom, even though she threw me out. I'm loyal to Camden, even though we're only married so he can have health insurance. I'm loyal to so many people and things beyond the time that they serve me... because I want them to love me.

I sigh again and snuggle in closer.

"What do you need?" he asks. "A drink of water or something stronger? Go home and sleep? Watch something on TV? Bang on metal?"

I giggle. "Bang on metal?"

Cam shrugs. "My dad used to call it that. You know ... go out in the backyard and get out the stress."

"I think I just want to go home and curl up with you. Is that okay?"

"Of course it is," he says, sounding mildly offended. "I like to be touched. Always have. And I like touching you."

"I like it when you're affectionate. I never had that kind of affection."

"And you were just starving for it, weren't you?" he murmurs.

I want to deny it, or at least shrug and brush it off like it's no big deal, but I'm also kind of tired of hiding who I am. I'm tired of hiding my past. I like how I can be myself with Cam and he doesn't seem to judge me.

"I think so, yeah," I admit. "I didn't get it as a kid, so I'm looking for it now."

"Then I'm your man," Camden says. And I wish it meant more than it does.

* * *

Over the next week, Camden has more doctor's appointments and treatments, and he's booted up and under orders to put no weight on his foot. But he does have medical devices—a knee scooter thing along with the crutches—that make it so he's able to move around more easily.

He spent a weekend afternoon, along with Charlie, Reyna, Danny, and Alden, helping me move entirely out of Evan's place. Cam was there more for moral support than anything else. I didn't have that much stuff, anyway—more clothes and too many craft supplies. Cam carried out my vision boards, which were all in a huge envelope. I still had a key, so I texted Evan when we were going to come over, and he stayed away. We brought so many people so we'd have witnesses in case something went wrong. But everything went smoothly. It made me nervous that Evan was so quiet, but I returned the key in an envelope in the mailbox and said goodbye to that loser.

Cam is able to return to working, at least the jobs that don't involve ladders or him putting weight on his foot. Every day, he kisses me goodbye before he leaves for work. He kisses me when he comes home. He kisses me when we're making dinner on the hot plate in the cramped kitchen. He kisses me when we go to the grocery store.

And I'm more than okay with it. Most nights we sleep in the same bed. I usually end up crawling out of bed early and jerking off furiously in the shower so he doesn't feel weird about my boners. He gets morning wood, too, but I try not to notice.

Camden's always got his arm around me, and I love it. When we watch television, I sit next to him on the couch and snuggle into him. And I feel all these touch sensors lighting up. Cam will stroke my arm, making the hairs on it rise. He'll caress the back of my neck. Somehow, I guess because we're married, he feels like he can.

And I want him to.

I've never had this kind of platonic arrangement. Or sorta-platonic. Since we kiss and make out sometimes.

We just don't have sex.

And I ... want to.

Camden

A s my ankle heals, Shelby and I get into a rhythm of going to work and hanging out at home. I'm able to get some construction work done in the outside world—subcontractors and laborers are a blessing—so I have some money coming in and can pay the mortgage and other bills. Shelby keeps trying to pay rent, but I won't let him. I do accept his buying groceries, though, and we alternate being in charge of meals.

I spend time at the physical therapist, and while I say no to the bone stim procedure, I do get fitted for some very sexy (not) orthopedic shoes. The bruises disappear from Shelby's face, and he seems to be back to normal.

He's been looking for a place to move, but whenever we've gone to check one out, they're never okay. Either too expensive or sharing with sketchy people or not in a good part of town. I told him he can stay here, and I want him to.

And it's slowly becoming a place where he *can* stay. Over the course of a few evenings, I managed to get the drywall up and texturized and primed it for painting, so the place doesn't look like a complete disaster anymore—it just looks vacant, with little furniture and no flooring to speak of yet. Everything takes me three times as long as usual, but it's getting done eventually. In other words, things are going well.

There's a problem, though.

I'm more turned on than I've ever been in my entire life. Before Shelby moved in, sure, I'd masturbate sometimes. It wasn't a daily thing.

Now, though? I'm rubbing myself raw thinking of him—sometimes more than once a day—and I feel like the creepiest creep who ever creeped. He said he doesn't want to be my experiment, and I'm not going to push him.

Even though I want to. Because it's becoming more than an idle attraction. His smile makes me light up inside. I just like having him around. I like the way he feels in my arms when we sleep at night. And I like getting to know him. I'm finding out, more and more, that we have things in common. This afternoon, for instance.

It's Saturday, but I spent the morning working on a small demo job, and I come home to find Shelby sitting at the kitchen table, surrounded by construction paper and magazines. I'm hot and sweaty, and I yank off my hat, hang it up in the closet, and take off my shirt.

I don't miss that he eyes me from head to toe. Part ... no, most ... okay, *all* of me likes it. I escape to my bathroom and take a shower, covering my cast with plastic like I'm supposed to, then return wearing shorts and a tank top that has the sides sliced to the waist.

"What are you doing?" I ask, downing a glass of water.

Shelby grins. "Putting together a vision board of ideas for your house. And one for our firm holiday party."

I gape at him. "What?"

"Now that you're on the way to getting this house in shape, I thought you might like some ideas of what it could look like. And while I'm doing that, I'm picking out ideas for the firm." He shrugs. "Some people do Pinterest. I like scissors, glue, and tape."

I stand over him. "Do you make vision boards a lot?"

"Kinda. I do lots of crafts. I make cards and books and scrapbooks."

"Really? That's cool. What's the most recent thing you put on a vision board?"

He reddens. "Um. A million dollars."

"Fair. I want that, too."

"And, you know. A husband. A nice house. A lot of love."

"You really had 'a husband' on your vision board?"

"I did. I had the words and a picture."

"What did the picture look like?"

Shelby looks down at his lap and mumbles something.

I reach over and tilt his chin up. "What was that?"

"He was a brown-haired dude in jeans and a flannel."

I'm amused. "Okay. What did the house look like?"

"Weirdly, it looked like this one. With the same roofline and the retro neighborhood. I wanted the xeriscaping, to be super cool, and I wanted a pool, because I'm inconsistent." He grins. "Here, I'll show you."

Shelby trots off to the pool house and returns with an over-sized portfolio. He opens it up, and there are all kinds of posters in it with pictures from magazines, headlines, and even some drawings and writing. He bites his lip and pulls out one from the bottom. "This is the most recent one."

I study it, and sure enough, there's a guy on there who does resemble me. The house looks familiar, too. Then I look at the writing and scratch my jaw, hiding a grin. "Um, Shelby, how come it says 'anus'?"

"That's 'an us,' not 'anus.'" He shoves me. "You know. I want to be part of a couple."

"Sure." I kiss the top of his head and study the board. "Well, we're kind of an 'us,' but we're not getting anywhere near the anus ... Okay, how are we talking about this? Wow, somehow you're getting everything on your list."

He giggles at my hasty attempt to change the subject. "I don't have a million dollars or a lot of love."

"Yet." I pause. "Actually, I think you're wrong. You *do* have a lot of love. Everyone at Weston & Ramirez adores you. Even my grumpy brother."

He shrugs. "I'm the office gossip. They want to talk with me because I keep them informed about everything that's going on. When they aren't talking to me, I know something big is happening."

"Does that happen very often?"

"No," he admits.

"So all you need is a million dollars, and you have everything on your list."

"Sorta."

"Can I make one?" I ask, taking the seat next to him.

He looks surprised, but he nods. A lock of platinum hair falls into his eyes, and I brush it away. We both look at my hand.

"Sorry," I say. "Okay, so how do we do this?"

"I just go by feel. What images speak to me. I rip them all out, then I make up a collage."

"Sounds like fun."

He passes over a stack of magazines: *Architectural Digest* and various decorating magazines, plus some with different focuses, like *People, National Geographic, Out, Men's Fitness,* and *The New Yorker.* "Where did all these come from?" I ask. I haven't seen him get anywhere near this amount of mail.

"Noah and August said it's okay for me to take them from our reception when we get the new ones in. And I maybe snuck one from Dr. Logan." He holds up a *Pride* magazine. "Reyna says her friend works for this magazine back east. There's supposed to be a calendar coming out soon." Shelby waggles his eyebrows.

I snort and pick up a *Men's Fitness.* "This kind of cover model gives me a complex. I'm never going to have abs like that."

"Do you want them?"

"Not really. I think I'm in good shape, but I like to enjoy a hamburger every once in a while."

"You look good." His ears go red.

"Thanks. So do you." Now his cheeks match his ears.

I start flipping through the magazines. I go more slowly than Shelby, who tears through them at a rapid pace, only stopping now and then to rip a whole page out.

Pretty soon, I loosen up and am doing the same thing he is, pulling out not just photos of ideas for this house, but also places I want to visit, landscaping I think looks cool, and anything else that pulls me to it.

I haven't had this much fun in a long time. I like to make things, but these days I only do it for a living. And to be on Ad/VICE, I guess. But this—there are no expectations. It's fun and freeing.

When we both have big stacks of photos and headlines or quotes, Shelby pulls out two large pieces of poster board as well as scissors, glue, and tape, and I start arranging the images I've picked out. "I've torn out way more than I'll ever be able to fit, so I'm going by what feels good," I say.

"Hmm," he says, then looks over and grins. He's so damned cute. "That's perfect. That's exactly how this should be. Just whatever feels good."

We both complete our art projects, and when we're done, we compare them. I've pulled out photos of houses, landscaping, pools, and vacation spots. Also people holding hands, champagne glasses clinking, roaring fires, skiing. Shelby points to the image of a snowy slope. "You like to ski?"

"I try to go at least once a year. This year?" I sigh. "Maybe I'll be healed enough. I hope so."

"Interesting. You can find out a lot about people from what they put on their vision board."

"It's kind of a mess and kind of beautiful," I say.

"That's how most things are."

Shelby's cut out photos of a pool and a house again, books on a shelf and trendy haircuts. And rings.

"You're asking for a husband, even though you already have one," I tease.

He shrugs. "I like being married to you, but someday I want a real relationship."

That's perfectly reasonable. So why does it hurt when he says it?

* * *

The following Friday night, Shelby texts me.

SHELBY

> The office happy hour is going to One tonight.
> Want to come? Drinks and dancing?

I've been to One before, since it's the Weston & Ramirez hangout.

CAMDEN

> Sure, although I'm not sure I'm up for dancing

SHELBY

> <confetti emoji> I'll come home after work and
> pick you up. We'll go together

CAMDEN

> Sounds like a plan

Shelby walks in a little after five and claps his hands. "Come on! Get dressed!"

I look down at my jeans and T-shirt. "I am dressed."

He clucks his tongue. "Not for a club, you aren't. Hang on. Let me get ready, and then I'll help you."

I shrug and go to my room, thinking I might have a button-down shirt that could work. Ten minutes later, I'm sitting on my bed dejectedly looking at my limited wardrobe when my husband walks into the bedroom.

He looks utterly edible.

Shelby's wearing a tight fuchsia T-shirt in a metallic fabric. It's also see-through. He's paired painted-on white jeans with pointy silver shoes. He's put on a little eyeliner and some lip gloss, and it's all I can do to not grab him.

"Holy shit," I yelp.

"What?" Shelby looks around.

"No, it's you. You look amazing," I say. I'm still hobbling, so he comes over and straddles my lap, which I don't know how he manages in those pants. They must have some stretch or something.

He nuzzles my neck. "God, you smell good."

"So do you. I want to kiss you, but I don't want to mess up your makeup."

"Eh. I'll reapply." And he kisses me while I palm his ass.

Once we break apart, I groan. "I thought you wanted to go out tonight."

Shelby gives me one more kiss, then gets up. "Okay, so ... need some help?"

I nod. "I'm pretty much jeans and T-shirts."

"That's okay," he says. "I like that look on you. But let's put you in one that's more fitted than usual. Okay?"

"Whatever you want."

He digs in my dresser and pulls out a plain black V-neck T-shirt that's on the smaller side, and I put on my best jeans and a heavy belt.

"I pretty much only have boots," I say.

"That's okay." Shelby finds a pair of black Converse. "Wear these. Or, well, wear one of them."

It seems good enough, so I get dressed. I study my face in the mirror. "I should probably shave," I start to say, but he cuts me off.

"Don't you dare." Shelby rasps his fingers across my stubble.

"This is so sexy. Oh my god, every man in there will want you. And you're mine. Come on!"

We take an Uber to One. Since it's still early, it's not packed yet, although there is a small crowd. We find our way to an upstairs room—taking the elevator rather than risking the stairs—and meet up with the rest of the crew.

I know many of Shelby's coworkers from hanging out with my siblings, but I've never met Weston & Ramirez's newish, most famous attorney, Sam Stone, or Sam's exponentially more famous boyfriend, Julian Hill. Sam's grandfather is the governor of California. Julian is an incredibly popular singer. Both are here tonight, and I'm frankly starstruck to meet Jules. There are two big guys in black standing nearby, and I bet they're his bodyguards.

Shelby sits me down and introduces me to both of them.

Jules shakes my hand. "Are you a friend of Shelby's?" He's got a great British accent.

"He's my husband," Shelby chirps, holding out his hand and showing off his ring.

Jules looks surprised. "When did you get married, Shelby? And you didn't invite us?"

"Oh, we eloped." He grins and climbs into my lap, kissing my cheek. I wrap my arm around him to hold him in place. "I couldn't wait."

Part of me wants to explain the circumstances, but I guess it's none of their business, or anyone else's. More importantly, I'm really starting to want those circumstances to change. I don't want to end our relationship once I'm healed and have my own health insurance or he finds another place to stay. Shelby brings a zest to my life that I'd been missing. He's creative and caring and efficient and clever.

The server, a woman everyone seems to know, comes up and asks everyone what they want. When she gets to me, her jaw drops. "Who is this?" she asks Shelby, her tone accusatory.

"This is my husband, Camden. He's also Charlie and Reyna's brother."

"Oh my god, Shelby! Husband? Congratulations to you both! Have a drink on me—what do you want?"

We both order beers, and she returns soon with everyone's drinks. This room isn't too loud, and we chat with Jules and Sam about the new album Jules is working on, their recent trip to Mexico, and how Sam is going to rent out his condo, now that he's been living with Jules on the beach for a while.

"How much is the rent?" Shelby asks, and I stiffen. "Asking for a friend."

"I don't know yet. I need to talk to a realtor and find out what's reasonable," Sam says.

"Okay, well, let me know when you do, so I can pass on the info."

I tighten my arms around Shelby, who is still in my lap, and mutter in his ear, "You don't need to find a place fast, you know."

"Yeah but I bet Sam's place is nice," he whispers back. "Probably too expensive, though."

"I'm struggling here, because I don't want you to go," I admit.

He turns and kisses me. "Then I'll drop it." But I can hear the "for now" implied in the statement.

After he finishes his drink, Alden and his boyfriend, Danny, come up and ask us to dance with them.

I gesture to my foot. "No dancing for me, I'm afraid."

Jules and Sam smile. "We'll keep you company."

"Go on," I tell Shelby, although I'm conflicted. I want him to have fun, but I'm feeling massively protective.

They head downstairs to the main floor, but from where I am, I can see him dancing with a group of guys from the firm. I mostly relax.

After a few minutes, a burly guy comes up and says something in Shelby's ear, but he holds up his hand, showing his ring. The guy says something else, with a lascivious look, but Shelby shakes his head no.

"Do I need to go down there?" I mutter. I'm already making my way to get out of the chair and over to the elevator.

Jules puts a hand on my bicep. "I think your husband can take care of himself."

"I know he can, but I don't want him to need to."

Just then, Shelby cranes his neck, looking for me. When he finds me, he waves excitedly, and I sit back down.

I can trust my husband.

Sam looks at me sympathetically. It seems he saw something in my expression that I didn't realize was there. "That's one of the tough things about being in a relationship. You have to believe that they really want to be with you."

Jules reaches over and squeezes his hand on the top of the table. "Even when the world is telling you something else. Or even when everyone outside of your relationship has an opinion about it."

But what about the opinions of those actually in the relationship, when you've agreed it should have an expiration date?

I decide not to think about it and instead to try to figure out a way to let Shelby know that I'm not in any hurry to end things with him.

And I'm kind of talking ... *ever*.

CHAPTER 14

Shelby

On Monday, I go to lunch with Alden. "Why are you looking so sad?" he asks, when we get seated at our table.

"It's complicated."

He smiles. "Try me."

"So, okay. You know why Cam and I got married."

Alden gives me a look. "Yes, I do."

I scrub my face. "What you don't know is that ..." I stop. Outing someone without their permission isn't acceptable.

But is it outing when he's married you and introduced you to random strangers and his family as his husband? When he kisses you in public? When the whole office sees you sitting in his lap at the club and canoodling?

It might still be.

This is confusing.

Alden waits patiently for me to go on.

"This is confidential."

He nods.

"In Camden's family, he's always been the straight one. He married me, sure. He doesn't have any homophobia—at least not that I can tell. But then he told me he's 'straight-ish.' And he's curious. He wants to, you know. See if he's into guys or not."

"By experimenting with you?" Alden asks.

"Yeah." My voice cracks. "I don't know if I'm okay with that."

"Because you don't want to do, y'know, stuff with him?"

"No, nothing like that. I want to. Believe me, I want to." I shiver. "I think he's so sexy. I've just had a lot of bad luck."

Alden furrows his brows. "Hasn't he shown he's a good guy?"

I chuckle wryly. "I realize it's a weird situation. I guess I feel like I'd still be a bi-curious dude's guinea pig, and I promised myself I wasn't going to get involved with any more unavailable men."

My self-esteem was in the pits when I was growing up, and I've been battling it ever since. So it figures Cam would be challenging me in the worst way on my deepest issues: on whether I'm worthy of a healthy relationship with a romantic partner. One step forward, two steps back.

"Hate to break it to you, but he's not unavailable if he's married to you and he's saying he's okay with messing around."

"Yeah, I see what you're saying. Okay. I'm being ridiculous."

"No, you aren't being ridiculous. You're guarding your feelings. If this marriage is just for insurance, you can walk away at any time. Or, rather, once he gets insurance on his own, you can say goodbye, like you planned. But if you start, I don't know, *liking* each other, that would make it more difficult."

"Especially since I usually fall harder."

"That's the real problem, isn't it?"

I nod. "He's been hurt before, too." I'm thinking of how publicly he got left at the altar.

"Just making sure—you told him you were okay with kissing?"

"Yeah. But now I want to do more. And he wants to do more. And I don't know what to do."

"In other words, you want your husband to do what husbands do."

"Right."

He takes a bite of his sandwich. "Okay, you two have been talking about it, though. Right? You have open communication?"

"We do."

"And you're not hiding anything from each other?"

"Not that I know of. He's told me some sensitive things about his history. I don't get the idea he's being anything other than straight with me. Ugh. Pun not intended."

"What would you want in the abstract? If you didn't let your fears hold you back. Would you want to sleep with him?"

"We've sort of done that."

Alden tilts his head. "I'm so confused. I thought that's what you wanted to do with him."

"We've literally *slept*. What I want to do is get him naked and do very naughty things with and to him while we're both awake." My voice drops. "Alden, do you realize he has pierced nipples? Pierced!"

"Ah." He waves a hand and almost tips his drink over. "Same question, then."

"If I weren't so scared of getting hurt, I would want to climb Camden Cooper like a tree."

"Then there's your answer."

Is it? "It can't be that simple. I'll end up being crushed."

"Or you could end up very happy. You're projecting that you're going to get hurt, but you have no evidence except your history. You create your future, and it doesn't have to repeat the past."

"You've been hanging out with too many lawyers."

"Only one in particular." Alden grins, surely thinking of Danny. "My advice is as follows: Talk with Camden about what he wants to do. See if you want to do it, too. If you do, let yourself do it without fear. Worrying is just a habit, like anything else. But in this case it's a habit you've developed based on being with, pardon my French, a bunch of assholes. If you don't think Cam is an asshole—and it certainly seems he isn't—then you can decide not to worry, because this isn't the same situation as the ones where you ended up getting hurt."

I stare at him.

"What?"

"You're so smart sometimes."

Alden smiles shyly.

"Thanks," I say. Which is a very small word to cover the fact that I now have a kernel of hope that I might be able to have what I want.

* * *

When I get home from work, Cam is sitting on the couch, hair wet from a shower. He looks up and smiles when I walk in. I don't know what to do, so I stand there, indecisive, long enough that it gets awkward.

"Want to watch something?" he asks.

"Yeah," I croak. In reality, I want to curl up on top of him. And it isn't even sexual. Or, at least, it's not *only* sexual. I just want to touch him. He's raw and powerful, but he smells good. He exudes strength, even with his injuries. Or maybe because of them.

And maybe because of them, it seems like he can handle anything.

Plus, he pays so much attention to me. He makes me feel like I'm his entire world. It's *wonderful*.

I sit rather primly off to the side, but he looks at me, rolls his eyes, and opens his arms. "C'mere."

I pounce. There's no other word for it, but I'm not going to look a gift Camden in the mouth. He's *mine*. I curl into him, and he's so fucking snuggly for someone so muscular.

Camden holds me a lot. He'll put his arm around me when we're waiting in line. He comes up behind me and hugs me and nuzzles my neck when I do the dishes.

Now, though, I want to touch him in the naked sense. My heart starts beating faster, and my cock thickens, because he's so damned sexy. That tousled hair and the scruff on his defined jaw. The way his biceps flex without him even trying. The bulge in the front of his jeans. The vibe he gives off of being effortlessly sure of himself—and that he'll take care of everyone around him. Like a true alpha male, not beating his chest and posturing, but doing what he has to to make sure the people he cares about are safe.

"How was your day?" I ask. I need to talk to him, like Alden suggested, but I don't know how to start. I don't want to scare him off.

"No jobs today, so I did nothing but nap. It's—my day—getting better now," he murmurs, kissing the top of my head.

The affection he shows me is something I never realized I needed, but now that I have it, I know I'd always been missing it.

Funny how if you grow up without something, it takes a bit before you learn that you were supposed to have it.

Now that I have it, though, I don't want to let it go.

"I talked with Alden today," I start.

"Hmm? What about?"

Might as well just say it. "About how I've changed my mind."

He sits up and looks at me. "About what?"

"About experimenting with you. Letting you be bi-curious with me, I mean. I guess I'd rather it be with me than someone else."

A slow smile spreads across his handsome face, and it takes my breath away. "Really?"

I nod. "And for what it's worth, I snuck in for STI tests after Evan, and I'm negative."

"Me, too. I asked for a physical, since I have insurance now, thanks to you. The doctor did a series of panels."

"Cool," I say faintly.

One of his hands plays at my hip, and I move so I'm straddling his legs. He moves a tentative hand so he's cupping my ass, and I almost groan in relief. Then he traces up and down my torso with a calloused finger. "You are so beautiful."

Now it's my turn to grin. "Thanks. I'd like to take credit for it, but it was all my mom and dad."

"No, much of it is you. Your choices in how you do your hair, how you take care of yourself and present yourself. But it's more than that—your good heart and positive attitude shine through. Guess all I'm saying is, I appreciate it."

"Thank you. It goes both ways, you hottie." Cam's attention on me always makes me feel gorgeous and wanted. It's heady stuff.

But now that I have the go-ahead, I need to clarify a few things. "So, if you still want to explore, I hate to be blunt," I say, "but I'm up for anything except for some stuff that's likely not on your to-do list anyway. So ... now you're the one calling the shots here, hubby. I'm yours. How far are you comfortable going?"

I like saying that I'm his. I like belonging to someone. Even if it is for our own weird reasons.

"For starters, I'm good with this," he says. And he cups my face and leans in to kiss me, his hand sliding down to palm my dick through my pants.

CHAPTER 15

Camden

Shelby kisses me back. His soft, insistent lips feel amazing against mine. He tastes good, and I love kissing him.

I want to do more with him, so if he's giving me the green light, I'm going to take him up on it.

Instead of pulling back like I usually do, I move him so he has no choice but to lie down on the couch, and I settle over him, my hips between his knees. I nuzzle his neck with my nose. His breath hitches, and he clutches my back.

"I want this more than you know," he whispers fiercely.

"Me, too. I think you are very, very sexy."

He looks up at me with trusting dark brown eyes. Then he nods. "Just promise we can talk afterward. I'm not usually an 'I need to talk about it' person when it comes to, you know, sex. But with you, it's different."

"Because it's my first time with a man?"

"Because it's between me and you."

"Yeah," I say, sucking on his neck. "I get it. I'll talk. We'll talk this whole time. Do you know how good you taste?"

"Unggh," he moans, and his hand starts to explore down my

back until he's gripping my ass. I try a few experimental grinds against him.

The breath that whooshes out of him makes me even harder. *Finally, we're doing this.* There are so many things I want to do, I don't even know where to start. Suck his cock. See the way he reacts when I touch him. Hear his moans.

I'm really fucking attracted to my husband.

"Come to bed," I murmur, and he follows me as I limp down the hallway on my crutches. It occurs to me that this isn't even primarily about me anymore. I want to make this worth it to *him.* "I want to drive you wild and for you to be happy we're doing whatever we end up doing."

"Oh, god," he whispers, as we both climb onto the bed. "Do your worst. Whatever you have planned, I'm good."

"I don't have a plan. Other than touching as much of your skin as I can. And making you come."

"Fuck." He starts shoving at the hem of my T-shirt, and I quickly take the hint and strip it off. His eyes widen as he looks at my naked torso. "You're so fucking hot," he says.

"So are you." I crouch down and lift the hem of his T-shirt with my teeth. Then I start slowly kissing up his belly, rucking up the shirt as I go. I lick one of his nipples, and he shivers and claws at my hair. He swallows and nods, then helps me take off his shirt.

I lower myself down onto him, and now we're skin to skin, kissing. His hands are all over my back, dipping into my waistband. His dick is hard against mine, and although it's a new sensation, I like it. A lot. It feels decadent and super erotic. It feels like I'm doing something naughty—which is ridiculous, since he's my husband and he's told me this is okay with him, more than okay. I kiss his mouth and then pull back and kiss more of his skin—whatever I can find.

Shelby starts shoving at my jeans. I unbutton and unzip my pants, but before I shove them down, I undo his as well, wanting to see him. His pants are tighter than mine, so I shift and let him take them off. He slides his underwear down, too, and then he's naked under me.

"You're so beautiful," I whisper. And he is. He's lithe and soft-skinned, with very little body hair. I wonder if that's how he is naturally. I think I wouldn't mind more hair, but either way, I like *him*.

"Let me see you."

I nod and stand up, dropping my jeans and underwear and kicking them off. My hard dick bobs out in front of me.

He inhales sharply. "Fuck, you're so hot. Come here."

"I'm not used to being bossed around in bed," I mock complain as I settle over him again, and fuuuuck, this feels good. My warm, naked body against his. Our cocks next to each other, trying to get friction. I'm kissing him and moving my hands all over him, and he's doing the same.

"I could come like this," he warns. "From the frotting, I mean."

"Do you want to?"

He shrugs. "I want to come, but I don't care how."

"Can I suck you?" I ask. I've always loved oral sex with women, giving and receiving. I think the feeling of a tongue down there is unbelievable.

"Are you sure?"

I've never even held a dick other than mine, but no time like the present. For some reason, I don't hesitate. I grin wickedly and answer by scooting down and licking up his length. I inhale his scent—a sweet combo of faint musk and body wash. Shelby's proportionate, so he doesn't have a monster cock, but it's not tiny, either. Smaller than mine, but he's smaller than me everywhere.

It's cute. Like him.

After another lick, I hold my breath, open my mouth, and swallow him down.

He arches off the bed with a muttered, "Fuck, Camden. What are you .... Okay, you are. Oh my god. Yes. Fuck. Yes. Please."

I grin around his dick and keep going. I make a quick decision that if he comes in my mouth, I'm good with it.

Growing up around gay guys, I heard them talking about it. And it's just spunk, after all. I've tasted my own. Who hasn't?

I start sucking him in a steady rhythm, but he shoves at my shoulders, so I pull back and look up. "What?" I ask, wiping my mouth with the back of my hand.

"I was going to come too fast, and I wanted to warn you."

I smile at him. "I don't mind."

"Well, at least let me return the favor. At the same time?"

I shiver. "Okay."

He flips around so his head is at my cock, and I reach out and stroke his dick. I lean in for a lick, and he gasps and then swallows me down, and I lose the plot entirely.

I'm getting sixty-nined by my husband, and I'm in heaven.

Shelby is an expert. I've never had someone be as thorough as he is, and his skills are seriously blowing my mind. And, ahem, my dick.

Why haven't we been doing this the whole time?

All too soon, I'm about to come, and I pull off his dick. "Wait," I say. "I want to keep going. I don't want to finish yet."

"You can fuck me," he pants. "If you want."

Oh my god. I do want. I want so badly.

But while I'm no prude—and certainly no inexperienced virgin—fucking Shelby right now feels like too much. I can't expect to be perfect right out of the gate.

"I want," I say. "But I'm not ready yet."

"Oh." He stiffens. "I'm sorry."

"No. Don't fucking be sorry. I want you more than you know. But ..." I bite my lip. "I want to learn what you like."

He knifes up and kisses me. "I'll have something to look forward to."

"That you do." My heart feels so warm right now. I arrange us so I'm again between his legs, kissing him and rubbing my cock against his. I don't think I've ever been harder than I am right now. Everything about Shelby turns me on. I love the way he feels against me and the way I feel when I'm with him.

"Stroke us off," Shelby whispers, and he reaches out a hand in the direction of the nightstand. I get the idea and lean over, fumbling for my trusty bottle of lube. Once I accomplish my mission, I pour some into my hand and wrap my fingers around his dick, and he groans out a husky, "*Fuck*, Cam."

I suck on his neck and keep stroking his dick, focusing on the tip, where I like it, on the assumption that he will, too.

Seems like I'm right, because right away, he's squirming, and his breaths are shallow. He's going to come.

Yes.

"You're mine, do you hear me?" I whisper.

He nods and moans.

I feel this huge sense of accomplishment as I make him tip over the edge into bliss, his face thrown back and his spunk jetting over my hand as he comes.

When he settles, I grin at him. "You're so sexy."

He gives me a shy smile back, then reaches down for my cock. "Let me."

I nod and lie on my side, and he spills out some more lube. Soon enough, I'm coming by his hand. I'm lost in the bliss of it all, my body quivering and the deep relief of an orgasm washing over me.

Once I've come down from the high, I flop onto my back and chuckle. "We're a mess."

"Yeah," he says breathlessly. "Let me fix that."

Shelby slides off the bed and returns with warm washcloths. After we clean up, he gets back into bed, but he's gone tentative. Biting his lip, leaving a few inches of space between us.

I'm having none of that. I haul him to me. "Come here, you."

Shelby snuggles happily into me, his back to my front. He fits in perfectly in my arms, and he sighs.

"I liked that a lot," I whisper.
"Me, too."
"Do we need to talk about it? We said we would."
"Nope. I'm good," he says.
"Yeah. I am, too."

CHAPTER 16

Shelby

When I get to the office the next day, Alden stops by my desk and gives me a searching look. "How are you doing?" he asks carefully.

"Fine."

He narrows his eyes.

I relent. He doesn't even have to say anything before I start blabbing. "I had a good night last night, okay? Cam and I got closer than we were before, and now I'm scared that I like him for realsies, and that is not something that was planned, but it's so me that of course it has to happen that way. Even if I don't want it to."

"Why don't you want it to?"

"Because he's ... not really mine. I'm not even sure what we're doing isn't still just an experiment for him."

Alden puts a hand on his hip. And again, he doesn't have to say anything before I'm talking all over him.

"Okay, okay. He wasn't acting very straight, and he says all kinds of things that make my heart go thump, but can I trust them?"

Alden gives me a look. "We talked about this."

I sigh. "I know."

In the heat of everything, he said I was his, which sounded like a chorus of angels singing. The only thing I've ever wanted was for a man to say I was his—and mean it. To want me that much. To protect me.

Cam feels like the kind of person who could do that. He's a protector, and he's someone who wants to be loved. I can tell that.

"I'm scared," I admit.

"Why?"

"While we didn't do a honeymoon, because it's not like that with us, this still feels like a honeymoon period. He's just too wonderful. I'm waiting for something to go wrong."

He huffs. "Why do we always do that? I did that when I was worried things wouldn't work out with Danny. I kept waiting for things to go bad. Just once, I want us to be looking for things to be amazing. For it all to work out in our best interest. For it to just get better and better and better. I know it's natural to want to protect yourself from getting hurt—but good things do happen, and you can't protect yourself so much that you cut yourself off from that possibility."

I smile at him. "You're right. Maybe I can withhold judgment. I want to stop reliving my old patterns."

"Old patterns die hard. I know how it is."

I give him a hug. Alden is one of the sweetest guys I know. He's no longer the virgin boy I met, but he's kept his sweetness with his makeover.

He's still himself, only in a nicer package, and it's terrific to see. It's also great to see him get his happy ever after. I just wish I could.

Except ... Cam and I have a bargain, and I should keep my end of it. My insurance is a stopgap for him, and I said I'd help him find something long-term. So when Demi stops by, I ask her the name of our insurance broker so I can get Cam some quotes.

"I thought you liked our coverage," she says, tapping on her iPad.

"Yeah, but I want to give a friend some options."

She agrees and gives me the contact info.

Why do I feel like I'm betraying Cam when I'm doing exactly what we agreed I'd do?

* * *

That evening, I putter around the kitchen, pulling out plates and setting the table. Cam throws together a casserole, then excuses himself to go take a shower before we eat. Because he works outdoors, he'll often take a shower when he gets home, not first thing in the morning like I do.

Ugh. When the two of us are together—even though his house is still a work in progress—it feels so domestic and wonderful. I've always wanted the easy camaraderie with a partner where we make a house a home.

Which is not what I had with my mom growing up. Oh, sure, she was around, but dinners were huffy affairs. She'd ask me a few questions about school in a perfunctory manner, but that was it. As for my dad, it's not like I did more than meet him on a few occasions.

With Cam, though, it feels like he genuinely cares about me. When he cooks, he thinks about my preferences and makes sure to not add too much garlic, because he knows I don't like it. And when he asks me about my day, he looks me in the eyes and asks follow-up questions, and it feels like he's really listening to the answers.

In short, I don't know what to do with myself. I'm starting to really care for Cam, and that's a no-no in my fucked-up life. Our relationship is based on convenience. Underlying that is the unspoken agreement that we shouldn't do anything to make it more difficult to cut and run when the time comes to divorce.

But I'm going to make the most of being with him while I can. I know it's a fine line to draw, but if I can have him physically, well, at least I have part of him, at least for now. I can worry about the future when it gets here.

When I hear the shower turn off, I glance at the timer for the casserole and get ideas. I skulk into the bathroom and grin darkly at Camden as he stands on the bath mat, drying himself with a white towel.

"What are you doing?" he asks, a note of amused suspicion in his voice. He wraps the towel around his waist, hiding his assets.

"I dunno," I say teasingly. I come up behind him and rub my cock against his terry-cloth-clad ass. "I kind of like the view." Reaching around, I run my hands up his abs, and he bites out a moan. I can see his cock start to thicken under the towel.

I tweak his nipples, tugging on those hot-as-fuck piercings, then go up on my tiptoes to bite at his shoulder. Cam shudders and tilts his head back. "Shelby," he groans. "You always make me so hard."

"That's the idea." I push at his hips until he turns to face me, and then I drop to my knees. "Let me," I whisper.

"Okay," he says, running a hand through my hair and letting the towel fall to the floor.

I open my mouth and swallow him down. His cock isn't fully erect, but it gets that way fast, and I love having it fill in my mouth.

He touches me affectionately and cradles my jaw. I love the contrast between his stiff shaft and the springy area of the head. I love how when I suck on it, I can almost bring him to his knees.

I brace myself against him, holding his thighs, and with a nod, I encourage him to fuck my face. I want to be used. I want him to get off on me.

I want him to be mine.

I hold his ass and spread him a little bit, then pull him down my throat. I let him thicken even more in my mouth, and soon enough, he's thrusting for real.

"Fuck, Shelby. I'm going to come."

I look up at him, locking my eyes on his and hoping I communicate it's perfectly okay.

"Wait," he says. "I want to see you come, too."

I pull off and tear my pants open, fisting my own leaking cock. His hungry eyes rake over me.

My spit drips off of him, and it's obscene, and I love it. I jerk myself and go back to sucking on him, and I'm coming fast, even faster than he is. I let Cam use my face, and he unloads.

I love the burst of seed sliding down my throat. I love how it tastes. I love that I made him come. I love that it was so hot. I love

...

Yeah. Not finishing that sentence.

* * *

After dinner, Cam is frowning at his phone as I flip through the television offerings, searching for something to watch.

I kiss his cheek. "What's that face for?"

He sighs. "Leah."

"Well, that's a way to ruin the mood."

Cam gives me an apologetic smile. "She's hounding me about going to her wedding. I should block her or change my number. Not sure why I haven't."

"Inviting you seems kind of, I don't know, narcissistic. It's not as if you had an amicable breakup, after all."

"I know." He shakes his head. "I don't want to go, but she's right that our situation feels incomplete. I mean, I haven't seen or talked with her since she said no at the altar."

My back stiffens. "She's not going to ask you to get back together again, is she?"

He snorts. "No. She's marrying her high school sweetheart. Not sure I ever had a real chance against him."

"Then why don't you talk with her? Maybe you need closure, too." I shrug. "Go to the wedding if you need to go." I sound braver than I am, but it's the right thing to do—letting him get the emotional catharsis he needs. "I mean, if you can bring a plus-one, I'll come with you."

He chuckles, though it sounds a bit strained. "That would definitely convince her family she made the right choice walking out on me."

"Maybe. But who cares what they think."

Camden scrubs his face with his hands. "I'll talk with her. I guess I might like to know what happened."

It doesn't surprise me that he's all over the place. I'd be that way, too. While I don't want to push him to go, if he needs to, then he—or we, if he's okay with that—should go. Plain and simple. "There are healthier ways of getting over a relationship than going to her wedding."

"True." He sighs. "I'll see what I think after I talk to her. Because right now it's just perverse curiosity."

Better make light of this before I get down in the dumps. "If we go, we can talk about *Star Wars* OSHA violations the whole time."

"Are you ever going to let me live that down?"

"Nope."

His fingers are poised over the phone to text back. "You sure? About me talking with her, I mean."

"Yep. And about going to her actual wedding, if it comes to that."

Letting out a big sigh, he starts typing. "Okay, I'm telling her that one, before I decide if I want to go, I want to talk with her in person, and two, I'll only consider going to the ceremony if I can bring my husband. That should shut her up." Cam looks at his phone, dry amusement on his face. "Judging by the bouncing dots, it's not shutting her up. Yep. Nope." He holds out his phone for me to read.

LEAH

HUSBAND?

WTF CAMDEN?

He opens his arms and pulls me in so I'm sitting in his lap, then lets me watch while he types.

CAMDEN

I got married to a guy, yeah.

LEAH

Okay, that's random

CAMDEN

Not when it's the right guy

Cam nuzzles his nose into my neck and then follows it up with a kiss. I'm really not sure how I got this guy, but god, I want to keep him. He keeps typing.

CAMDEN

Anyway, thank you for the invite, but I want to talk to you first.

After, if you still want me to come, it'll be the two of us.

LEAH

Sure, he can come. Okay. Cool. This is different. Where do you want to meet?

CAMDEN

Southwinds Coffee in Sherman Oaks, Saturday at 10?

LEAH

Okay, see you then

He looks up at me. "Thanks for the push. I think this has bothered me for a year now."

I smile. "Sure."

And he kisses me again.

Camden

Saturday morning, I walk into the coffee shop on my crutches and look around for Leah. She's easy to spot, sitting by herself with a cup of hot tea in front of her. Her dark brown hair is in a sleek ponytail, and she's in simple jeans and a loose blouse, with sparkly sandals. All I can think is that she doesn't look anywhere near as enticing as my husband.

I suppose I can get this over with.

After I give her a chin-up nod of acknowledgment, I order at the counter and get my own coffee. Then I go over to her table. "Hey," I say, as I take the seat across from her.

"Hi," Leah says. She looks down at her hands, then squares her shoulders and stares me in the eye.

This woman caused me so much heartache. So much embarrassment. Cost me so much money.

And as I look at her, her long hair drawn over her shoulder, I'm finding it hard to muster the energy to be pissed anymore, or even to care at all.

Maybe it's because I've been pissed for so long.

"Small talk isn't really going to work," I say. "You called me here to talk. So talk."

She snorts. "Always the same, Camden."

I level her with a glare. So ... maybe I am still upset.

"Okay, fine. What I did was shitty, and I feel so bad about it that I can't move on from it."

"I have."

Leah nods. "Okay, yeah. I get that. And we need to talk about your *husband*. But with us, didn't you feel it, too? How we weren't clicking?"

"No. I thought it was just wedding stress."

"Wedding stress, sure, but ... if it was like that when we were planning the best day of our lives, what did it say about the worst?"

While I want to protest, I decide to shut my trap.

She keeps going. "It wasn't that I woke up one day and fell out of love with you. But I woke up one day and realized I didn't want to marry you. I didn't want to be with you my entire life. I'm sorry I wasn't able to tell you that before, well, the ceremony. But I don't regret the choice."

Well, if that isn't a kick in the dick. "Thanks."

"No, it's not you, and it's not me. We just weren't right together. Sometimes being together—the fact that we had history —isn't enough to mean you should stay together. Don't you think?"

I suppose she has a point. And I have the feeling that I dodged a bullet. Even though what she's saying hurts my pride at some level, I know I deserve better than someone who doesn't want to be with me.

I deserve someone like Shelby.

Leah sighs. "Also, if you got married so fast, and to a guy, maybe there were things that you weren't acknowledging, too. You know?"

While I want to deny it, she's right. I shrug. "Maybe. It was still a damned expensive wake-up call."

She has the decency to cringe. "Yeah. I know. Guess that's the other part of what I wanted to talk to you about. I want to pay you back for what we spent. I have a little saved that I can send to you."

I stare at her. The prideful part of me wants to tell her I can handle it, but that seems like I'd just be hurting myself. Or hurting myself *more*. Finally, I give her a curt nod. "Yeah, okay. Whatever you want to contribute, I'll accept."

This conversation isn't turning out to be the most comfortable one of my life, but it's also not the worst. And I'm realizing that I'm over her. I'm glad that we're not married, and I don't want to think about her ever again.

We keep talking, and she tells me about her fiancé and what they meant to each other in high school. I knew some of this, and I don't particularly care about the rest. But her ending up with him has some poetry.

"You and I weren't meant to be," I finally say. "You're right."

"So do you want to come to the wedding?" Leah gives me a wry grin. "I guess I thought that all those people I embarrassed us in front of might feel better if they see that we've both moved on and are in better places."

"Do we really need that?" I ask.

She pauses and looks off to the side, then turns back to me and shakes her head. "Maybe not. Maybe all I needed was to talk with you."

I let out a breath. Dodged another bullet.

Leah points at my foot. "So, what happened here?"

I choke on my coffee. "I, uh, hurt it. That's a long story."

* * *

"Hey. It's the weekend. Do you want to go do something? With me?" I ask my husband when I get home. He's finishing up the dishes.

"Sure!" Shelby wipes his hands on a dish towel and skips up to me, wrapping his arms around my middle.

His enthusiasm is infectious, and it makes me chuckle. I kiss the top of his head, then raise an eyebrow. "Don't you want to know where?"

"If it's with you, I'm sure we'll have a fun time."

I can tell he wants to ask me about Leah but doesn't want to push. I kiss him, then say, "Talking with Leah was better than I expected. We cleared the air. We agreed that we were both better off marrying other people."

He looks at me and nods slowly. "Okay, that sounds good."

I sigh. "Yeah, it was. I didn't want to talk with her, but when I saw her, I don't know. It was like she didn't matter anymore. There wasn't any spark. Unlike with you."

He blushes, but I'm very serious. Whenever I'm around him, I'm hyperaware of my body—how my skin tingles when he brushes up next to me, and I get this electric jolt when he touches me, even accidentally.

Also, he gets me sidetracked easily. "We could do something really exciting, like pick out paint for the house."

Shelby beams. "I'd love to help you with that." His face falls. "Do you want me to, though? I mean, this is your house. I've already overstayed my welcome—"

I cut him off. "No, you haven't. I don't want you to leave." He has no idea how true that is. "If you wanted to, we could finish fixing up my bedroom, and you could move inside with me. I mean, if it isn't too fast." I feel the need to backpedal, like maybe we aren't on the same page, but with his next words, he shows that he's with me.

"We did this all backward, didn't we? First move in. Then get married. Then ..." He waves a hand.

I nod. "Most of the time, people date first before making it formal with a wedding." I look to the side. "I do know I want you in my life, though."

"Good thing we're already married."

Do I want him to be in my life for real, though? Like, as my boyfriend, beyond our deadline?

A big part of me says yes. Even though I'm scared to be in a relationship, given how the last one ended, I'm so happy with Shelby that I'm willing to take the risk. He's the support I've always wanted, and he lets me take care of him, too. Not to be too cheesy, but just seeing his smile and enthusiasm can make my whole day. He's adorable in every sense of the word, and I'm pretty damned smitten. I want to wake up to him every morning and spend every night with him. I like the way his brain works, always planning and managing things for the future while enjoying the present. I like hanging out with him and doing everything and nothing.

And don't get me started on how hot he is. I fucking love that bleached hair and the curve of his ass and the way he fits against me.

Life feels better with Shelby. Period.

I just hope my heart can handle the fallout if this doesn't last.

* * *

Shelby and I walk around the Do-It Center, making dirty jokes the whole time. We're going to get flooring and paint for the house, but we keep getting distracted.

"Need some hard wood?" Shelby asks with an innocent expression on his face. "I think you can pick it up over there. Or do you need the right *tool?*"

I wrap an arm around his shoulder and mutter into his ear, "Don't you dare give me a boner."

"I'd never."

I snort. "Try *always*. You always turn me on."

He looks up at me and grins, and something in his smile rearranges my insides.

He's so cute in his bright purple polo shirt and tight jeans, and he gets excited about the smallest things. Like what kind of faucet I should put in the second bathroom. When we pass by flooring, he gasps. "That's gorgeous!" He points to tile that's a wood pattern, and yeah, he's right. It looks amazing.

"Should we order that? I'd like it to go throughout the whole house."

"I hate to ask, but I suppose I'm your husband: can you afford it?"

"Yep. I got paid for a big job, so I'm okay to put some into the house." I boop his nose. "And as you said, our home isn't habitable. We can't keep living like that. Come on, let's get it and then pick out paint." I pull out the measurements on my phone and place an order at the counter.

We head over to the paint section, and I stand behind Shelby as he chatters animatedly about paint chips. But all I can think of is how cute his ass looks when he stretches to reach some in the back.

"I'm not really sure how many times in my life I've been to Home Depot, hardware stores, lumberyards, flooring warehouses, and paint stores," I mutter. "But I've never been horny in one before."

His eyes widen, and he looks down, then bites his lip, discreetly rubbing my junk. "I really think we should go with this one for the living room, don't you?" he asks, holding out a very pale gold. "It looks like sunlight, and I think it would make the room so cheery."

I groan. "Then let's do it."

"In the Do-It Center." Shelby cocks his head. "That reminds me. I've been meaning to ask: did you use a stud finder on yourself, and did it go off?"

I snort-laugh. "It's like we're in high school and not reputable adults with real jobs," I say, adjusting my jeans. But I wrap an arm around his shoulders and kiss the top of his head. "Honestly, I've never had more fun."

"I want to help paint. Is that okay?"

"You don't have to, but sure. Let me tell Charlie, too. He'll want to be there."

We order paint, get it mixed, and leave, me shaking my head at how much more fun it was to take my husband to the store with me.

When we get home, I set up a camera on a tripod in the corner and put it on time-lapse. "Do you want to be in an Ad/VICE video?" I ask.

His eyes light up. "Do you want me in one?"

"I want to keep you all to myself, but it might be difficult to keep you out of frame."

"I'm in," he says cheerfully, and skips to come help.

We spread out drop cloths and prep to paint. Shelby is incredibly diligent, getting right to work taping off areas. Charlie shows up before long.

"Should I edge?" Shelby asks innocently.

Charlie looks between us. "Was that innuendo?"

"What? No. We don't innuendo," Shelby says, smirking. He's wearing one of my paint-splattered T-shirts, and he's drowning in it, but I can't stop touching him. Which is a problem when we're painting.

"So it was. Okay. I see how you guys are."

Only he doesn't, since he has no idea how Shelby and I are in private. I'm not sure I want to tell him.

Oh, it's not like Charlie would say something mean. But as I told Shelby, I want to keep him to myself right now. It almost feels like we're fixing up *our* house together.

As I pull out the extension roller and start laying down a coat of paint on the ceiling, Shelby cuts in on the edges and Charlie works a roller on the walls. Between the three of us, we make short work of the room and end up painting the hallway and the kitchen as well.

"Wow. A coat of paint makes a huge difference," Shelby says when we're done, as Charlie fiddles with the camera.

"It's great." Seeing this place come together makes me long for something more with him, so we can share it. I want a real relationship with Shelby, but that's not guaranteed, and it's not what we agreed on. Odds are I'm going to be here when he's gone, after we get a divorce, and I'm always going to think about him when I look at the design choices. I like the design choices, though, so I'm not sure there's any way around it. I guess I'll deal with that when it comes.

"When is the flooring going to come in?" Charlie asks.

"Tomorrow."

"Then I'll be back if you need me."

Shelby looks me over. "Maybe we should let you rest that ankle. We're not very good at keeping you off your feet."

"That's true," I admit.

"Does it still hurt?" Charlie asks.

"Kinda. It's more of a dull ache, and if I keep it immobilized" —I gesture to the boot—"I'm good."

"He wouldn't tell us if it's too much, would he?" Shelby asks Charlie.

"Nope," Charlie says. He studies me. "But staying still would drive you up the wall, wouldn't it?"

I nod. "I can't stay put."

"Promise me you'll tell me if you're in too much pain," Shelby says. "And that you'll take a break when you need to."

I don't really want to promise that, but I also don't want my ankle to get worse. I swallow. "Yeah, okay. I promise. I do think it's pretty well on the way to healing, and I don't put weight on it, even if I'm moving around."

Shelby looks mollified, and Charlie promises to pester me about it going forward.

Shelby insists on buying us all dinner—he runs out and brings back a bunch of tacos, which we scarf down—and then Charlie leaves and Shelby and I shower together. We can't keep our hands off each other. I kiss him under the water, needing to touch his naked skin.

"Turn around," I whisper, "let me work those muscles."

"You could do more than that," he says with a laugh, which turns into a smirk as I suck on the back of his neck and then give his shoulders and back a massage.

"Cam," he whines. "I need you."

I spin him around. "We're clean enough."

We hurry out of the shower, dicks hard, and race to bed, our bodies clean and worn out. And yet I still have the energy to make him come.

I've never wanted anyone the way I want Shelby.

And I want to keep him.

* * *

Over the next few weekends, we get the house into much better shape, and it feels like my life is coming together, too. After Leah, I'd torn everything apart, but now I'm rebuilding the way I want it to be. It doesn't quite look like I imagined it would. But no creative project ever does. I guess I just have to celebrate what shows up—and that goes for Shelby's and my relationship as well as the house.

It's dawning on me that Shelby and I feel real. Like he's my boyfriend. Like we're dating.

My front brain tells me that I should have some issue with that. I've never been with a man before. I used to identify as straight. Am I supposed to have a crisis?

I'm not going to have a crisis.

I like my husband-maybe-boyfriend. He's caring and resourceful. He handles things and is generous and chips in. So maybe we can keep this thing how it is between us?

When Charlie puts the new Ad/VICE video up, it gets a lot of views, as usual. I don't take that for granted—viewers can always go away—but for now, the CoopBros account helps us get a little bit of sponsorship money, and I use my portion to reinvest in the house.

What I'd anticipated—but hadn't fully appreciated—was how much interest commenters would have in Shelby.

"Who's the cutie pie?"

"OMG. Charlie, is that your boyfriend?"

"Does the twink come with the house?"

And so on.

I let most internet comments go, otherwise they'd bother me forever, but when it comes to Shelby, I want to put a fence around him with a sign on it that says MINE. I don't want anyone to say mean things about him, but I also don't want anyone else to desire him. And I certainly don't want any of them to think he's Charlie's.

Charlie, of course, thinks that all this is hilarious.

But he doesn't know how much I really like my husband.

CHAPTER 18

Shelby

I'm playing house with Camden, that's all there is to it. I'm living in this domestic fantasy I never really had, with a husband who loves me, a house that I get to decorate exactly how I want it, and many kinds of hot sex every night.

I'm lying on top of him on his—our?—*his* new couch in his newly painted living room that has baseboards and flooring and furniture and a few black-and-white digital prints of his family. He even put up a framed picture of me—a still from the Ad/VICE video where I have paint on my nose and am grinning widely at the camera.

It makes a lump lodge in my throat.

Right now, we're watching all the *Star Wars* movies we can find, and Cam's comments crack me up.

Examples: "I think not only does the Death Star need OSHA to come in and shut it down, but is there an HR for the Empire? Choking people is not how you should fire them." Or "Don't they know you don't need to bank turns in space?"

His indignation about the "realities" of a fictional world makes me laugh. It makes my heart sing, too, because I like spending time with him.

We could watch anything, and I'd enjoy hearing his commentary. When the movie ends, I hesitate to get up off of him. He's just too snuggly, and I don't really want to move. I look up, hoping he'll kiss me—and he does, but then he pulls back and looks at me cockeyed.

"What?" I ask, nibbling my lip.

"Are we dating?"

I'm so surprised that I stutter out a laugh. "What?"

Cam clears his throat and doesn't meet my eyes. "I realize that's a strange question to ask my husband. But are we dating? Is that something that you want to do, or consider us doing? How do we do this? I mean, I like you."

I put my head into the crook of his neck and trace patterns on his chest while my own heartbeat speeds up. "I'd like us to be dating. I like you, too."

"Then, cool. We are." He moves so now I'm on my back on the couch, and he's on top and kissing me.

Settling something like that so easily is foreign to me. I'm used to people not saying what they mean or not telling me the whole story.

I want to trust him. I want to think that everything is going to be okay. But I've learned that it never is. There's always a cost.

I guess I should just enjoy this time with him while I can. I'll worry about when the other shoe will drop another day.

For now, I'm going to make out with my boyfriend. Who also happens to be my husband.

* * *

A few days later, Alden and Danny get engaged at a World Series game, and I congratulate them wholeheartedly. But part of me feels a pang. Somehow what I have with Cam has gotten confused with the relationships I see my friends in. Cam and I went into this with no intention of staying together, but now he's my boyfriend.

Does that mean our end date is off the table? Well, we never had a specific date—it was just when he's healed and has insurance on his own, and I have a place to stay. Which reminds me that I haven't totally kept up my end of the bargain.

In between reserving a venue for our firm holiday party and sending out cute invitations to everyone, I do some apartment searches on the office computer when there's no one calling or in the reception area. Cam and I have looked at a few places, mostly at the beginning, but so far nothing's been right. Likely because I don't want to move. I want to stay with Cam.

But that's not fair to him. Even if we're boyfriends, living together should be something he thinks about and actually wants, not because it was a spur-of-the-moment offer when he got hurt and I lost housing. I don't want him to feel trapped or like he can't get rid of me.

I learned, too, from Reyna, that he'd intended to rent out the pool house as an Airbnb. So I'm costing him income as well. I know it's offset some by the insurance premiums, but that can't be as much as he'd make with a rental.

Part of me also needs a backup plan. I didn't have one with Evan, and I paid the price. I'm not going to do that again.

The insurance broker Demi put me in touch with emails me a variety of plans tailored for small businesses, and I hesitate. I could forward them to Cam.

But I don't want to, because it feels like we're headed to the end if I do.

So instead, I print them out and put them in a folder. I'll put everything together for him, and we can talk about it like adults.

Just not today.

* * *

Early in the morning on November 5, my phone rings. *Ugh.*

"What's that?" Cam asks, his voice bleary. While he's an early riser for his construction jobs, he sleeps in on weekends.

"No one. Or, it's my mom. I'll get it."

He sits up fast. "Your mom?"

I nod. "She feels obligated to call." I answer my phone, trying not to wince, and Cam stretches out in bed, his bare torso inviting. While I could go somewhere else, I think part of me wants him to hear this conversation. I get a swoopy feeling of dread in my stomach, but I might as well get this over with.

I long for things to be different, but they aren't, and they won't be. So I brace myself for rejection at the same time I long for her approval.

And I do my best to lock down all these feelings.

"Happy birthday," she says, her voice audible in the room even though it's not on speaker.

"Thanks." My tone is flat. I glance over at Camden, and his eyebrows are raised. I didn't tell him that it was my birthday, and I'm sure he didn't memorize it from our marriage license application.

Mom says, "I didn't know where you were, so I didn't know where to send you a card."

I narrow my eyes. "I'll text you the address. But you don't have to send me a card."

"I think I do. It's expected." She sounds annoyed.

My chest aches, and I rub my face. I want to tell her that things she does out of a sense of duty are not things that I want. I want her to love me because I'm me, not because she's supposed to. And that's never going to happen. "Okay, thanks for calling," I say.

"Where are you living?"

I swallow a lump in my throat, wishing she really did care about where I am. "I'm in the Valley now." I'm not even sure she's listening.

"Good. And how is work?"

"Work is fine. I like my job and the people. I've been there more than eight years."

"That long?"

"Yeah. How is your job?"

"It sucks, but in ten more years I'll be able to retire."

That's a pet peeve of mine. If she hates it, why endure it for another ten years? That doesn't make sense to me, but it's not like we have the kind of relationship where we talk about things like that. After chatting with her a little bit, I get off the phone as fast as I can.

I realize when I hang up that I never told her I'm married. But I suppose we don't tell each other anything, big or small.

Cam sits up behind me and pulls me into his lap. All he's wearing are boxers, and he's moved down to a smaller brace on his ankle. "Few things," he mutters, kissing my neck. "That was your mom?" He reaches down and starts stroking my morning wood.

I nod and moan.

"And it's your birthday?"

I pull away. "Don't."

He holds up his hands. "I'm sorry. I didn't mean—"

I sigh. "It's not the touching me that's the problem. I'm sensitive to shit with my mom. And my birthday reminds me of her."

"You, who are so good at organizing and planning so many things, don't celebrate your birthday?"

"No. Not since I was eighteen."

Cam gives me a long look. "She fucking kicked you out *that day*?"

My nonresponse is response enough.

"Did you have any warning? Any place to go?"

I shake my head. My chest tightens, remembering how hard that first year was. The terrible rooms I rented that smelled of pot and cigarettes. "She gave me three thousand dollars and told me to use it as a security deposit. I already had the receptionist job at Weston & Ramirez. I'd been working there since I turned sixteen.

So I had a job and a little money saved, but I mostly used that for my car payments and insurance. Now, all of a sudden, I had to make rent, buy food, and all that."

I get out of bed and go rummaging in my dresser. I pull out an old card that I keep at the bottom and shove it at him. "That's the card my mother gave me on my eighteenth birthday."

He holds it gingerly. It's a standard store-bought card reading "Happy Birthday to My Son." On the inside, it says "From Mom."

"Not very sentimental, is it?" I say.

"Why the hell would you keep that?"

"To remind me not to get my hopes up. To remind me to keep myself in check, so I don't go around expecting anything from the world that it's not going to give me."

Cam's dark eyes take me in, and the shock I see in them unnerves me. "Babe," he says quietly, "come here."

While something in me wants to run away, I do what he says. This is Cam.

He opens his arms, and I crawl into his lap. He nestles his face in my hair and sighs. "I have so much to say to you, and I don't even know where to start."

"I have that problem a lot."

"I think you're incredible. You give so much to everyone else. You've helped me with the house when you didn't need to. You do things for the office that you don't need to. And if you're doing it all without expecting anything in return ..." He sighs again. "I love that you do things out of the goodness of your heart rather than as a transaction where you expect or demand payment of some kind. But I do think you need to realize that you deserve to be treated as well as you treat everyone else. Sometimes people who give and give don't ever let people give them things in return. It's like they don't think they deserve nice things."

I shrug. "I mean, yeah, sometimes. But I've let you buy me things. You bought our rings. You've bought me meals. You've given me a place to stay."

"And you give me so much more. You've given me my health. You've rehabilitated my home. You've given me a whole new understanding of myself. I don't know how I can balance that out, and I want to."

"Don't make me cry," I say.

"Yeah. Sorry." He swallows. "What if we make today an anti-birthday for you?"

"Nope."

"You say that too fast. But what if we do all the things you hate? We can do laundry, and eat tons of garlic, and watch true-crime shows—"

Despite myself, I crack up and tackle him. He falls easily onto his back, and I straddle his hips. I kiss his chest and between kisses say slowly, "I would be willing to make an exception this year, if we did things that we both wanted to do. Like, the intersection part of a Venn diagram."

"Do we know what those things are?" His voice is getting husky, because I'm sliding down his body, getting nearer to the waistband of his underwear.

"Guess we'll have to find out." I pop his now-hard dick out and give it a lick. "What do you say to blow jobs?"

"Well, I don't know," he says, pretending to think. "Are you sure *you* like them?"

I swirl my tongue around his tip, enjoying his warm, sleepy tone. "Let's see if it's in a place we intersect."

* * *

An hour later, we're showered, dressed, and on the road headed to a restaurant Cam likes at the beach. It's a clear fall day, and by the time we make it to the breakfast place, it's almost brunch time.

"What do you think about breakfast burritos?" he asks.

"That overlaps on the Venn diagram."

Cam chuckles. "That's a funny way of saying you like the same things I do."

"What can I say? I'm weird."

"I think you mean 'cool,'" Cam says, squeezing my hand.

We walk into the hole-in-the-wall restaurant, and a group of guys a little younger than me gasp when they see Camden.

"Oh my god, it's one of the CoopBros," one of them says.

Cam scrubs the back of his neck. "Yeah. Hey."

"Can we take a selfie, please?"

Cam shrugs. "Sure."

Then one of them recognizes me. "Wait, that's the guy from your latest video."

I wave. "Hey."

"That's my husband, Shelby. We got married this summer." The proud way Cam says it makes my heart soar.

"Oh my god, congrats," one of the guys says. "Shelby, can you get in the picture, too?"

After looking at their expectant faces, I give in. "Sure. Why not?"

We all crowd in, four of them plus the two of us, and Cam holds the camera because he's the tallest. After snapping off a couple of shots, Cam gives them back the phone, and we go to our table.

I'm absolutely thrilled that Cam claimed me in front of his fans.

"Do you get recognized often?" I ask.

He slides into the booth. "Sometimes. It happens."

At the table, we brainstorm things to do today. I make sure that whatever we do, he likes, too, but we still end up with quite a list: shopping for lamps, going to the La Brea Tar Pits, checking out the trains in Travel Town, and sitting on rooftops among them.

"Why do you like rooftops?" he asks. "From your reaction to the Ferris wheel, I thought you didn't like heights."

"That's different. It moved. Roofs stay put. When I was a kid, we lived in this apartment, and it felt like the roof was the one place where I could sneak off and get away from everyone. Like I had a place to go no one knew about, but I was still in the building. It was an alternate world."

Cam grins. "Same. I always like going on roofs. We'll have to go to a rooftop place for dinner tonight. Will that work?"

"Sure. Happy birthday to me," I mutter.

But despite my grumpiness, we do a lot of things on our list, and it ends up being a pretty spectacular day.

When we get to the restaurant for dinner, after spending the day all over Los Angeles, Cam gets a shy look on his face and hands me a gift bag he had stashed somewhere in his truck.

I furrow my brow. "When did you have time to do this?"

He chuckles. "Actually, I had this made a while ago, but I hadn't given it to you yet. So it can be a birthday present. Or, if you don't like it, an *anti-birthday* present."

Undoing the tissue paper, I pull out a dark blue T-shirt with text in yellow Futura font that says "Galactic OSHA Inspector." While my first reaction is to laugh hard, my second reaction is to swoon. Because Cam thought of me and had something custom made for me.

When people say it's the thought that counts, they mean things like this. It's just another way that Camden and I are starting to have inside jokes and shared memories and sex and legal consequences. In other words, what I think of as a real marriage.

There might be one thing missing from my list, though.

CHAPTER 19

Camden

It's the weekend, and I'm making out with Shelby in bed. This is becoming our usual, and you'd think I'd be getting used to how intensely I feel about him.

I'm not.

Don't get me wrong. I'm enjoying the hell out of being able to touch him. His body is so sexy—how he's masculine but not as big as me is a turn-on in a new and different way.

I want to throw him around a bit, but I also want to care for him. That's confusing.

What isn't confusing, though, is my body's reaction to him. When I kiss him for any length of time, I get aroused.

I reach down and squeeze his ass, pulling him closer as we explore each other's mouth. He makes these little moans that I'm not even sure he's aware of. Whimper-groans that turn me on even more.

I love it.

He runs a palm up my chest, lingering on the little silver barbells in my nipples, and as I tug him to me, he wraps that arm around me and hoists a leg up so we can get closer. Our cocks touch, and it's so fucking pleasurable I don't know what to do.

Getting myself off isn't good enough anymore. Something about the communion with him is just better. It's awesome.

Soon I'm pushing him back and settling between his legs, rubbing against him like a cat against a piece of furniture. And he's whispering, "Camden. God. That feels so good."

"I want to make you come."

"Oh, don't worry. You will." I've never had a partner as into it as Shelby is, and it makes me so fucking happy.

Plus, oh, he's my husband, which adds a whole other level to this. Like we're invisibly bonded.

I need to be careful, though. I can enjoy him now, but it's starting to feel like he's mine permanently. And that's a dangerous thing for me to think, because it's not true. We're coming up on ten weeks of marriage, and my ankle is almost healed.

His lips nudge my neck while his hand explores my torso. His weight against me feels so fucking good. "I really want to ride your dick," Shelby says, panting.

A cocktail of apprehension and excitement bubbles through my veins, and I try to calm my fear. I put the brakes on having anal sex when he originally asked, because I wanted to learn what he liked in bed first. Not that anal is some kind of goal or the One True Sex or anything. I just needed some time. But now I'm ready for it, too.

"How did I guess you were a bottom? Or are you vers?" I nibble on his neck.

"Hey, you know the terminology." He thrusts so his cock rubs against mine, and we both groan.

"Queer siblings." My breaths are getting ragged.

So are his. In between pants, he gets out, "I wasn't expressing surprise. It's acknowledgment that you've been exposed to more gay culture than the average bear."

"I'm not a bear," I say, and he laughs, then moans.

"You got it right. I'm mostly a bottom."

We keep kissing, and kissing, and kissing. "I'm ready," I whisper. "If you still want me to fuck you."

"I do," he murmurs immediately. "I'm good to go."

Time to admit a few fears. "I'm afraid I'll get inside you and come immediately. But I do want to fuck you."

"If you come, then you do. We'll simply have to practice again," he says with a sexy wink. "I say you should go for it."

I don't know if we're going too fast or not fast enough. I don't know if we're going from zero to sex and should slow down. I just want to fuck my husband, date him, and kiss him lots, and if that's a strange order of operations, so be it.

Sometimes you prepare as-built plans after you construct something, because it isn't what was originally envisioned. I hadn't planned on being a husband to a man or for Shelby to be in my life, but I am digging this so much. I'm going to have to create as-builts for my life.

"Let me prep," he says, reaching for the lube.

"I can do it for you." I take the bottle from him and pour some into my hand. Then I lift his legs up and gently probe his hole with a finger. He's so hot and tight. It's going to be amazing to fuck him. "You're gorgeous, and you're going to feel so good on my cock."

He shivers. Loosening him up feels intimate and sexy. It feels like I'm taking care of him, and I *want* to take care of him.

As I get him ready to take me, I kiss him, and he whimpers, kissing back. Pretty soon, he's batting my hand away. "I'm ready. Fuck me. I want to lose myself in you."

"I can do that."

While I'm maneuvering my hard, throbbing dick to his puckered entrance, he catches my eyes. "I'm serious," he says. "Use me."

I lube up, probably too much—I haven't had anal often in the past, so maybe I'm going overboard, but whatever—and start pressing into him. "You still okay with no condom?"

"Yeah. Definitely."

"Cool. Me, too." It takes a little force to breach his first ring, and then we both stare at each other, blinking. He's holding his breath, so I tell him, "Breathe, baby."

He nods and tugs my hips. I want to slam inside, but it's not that easy. I'm sure it stings. Women have told me so. I don't want him to be any more uncomfortable than he has to be.

Shelby bites his lip, and I enter him farther, bit by bit, until my balls nestled up to his ass. "Oh my god," I groan. "You feel incredible."

"Same," he pants as I pause to let him adjust. "Fuck, that's amazing. You fill me up, and ... fuck."

That's what I need to do. I do an experimental pull out and thrust in, and he nods some more. "Okay. Go. It's okay."

I still worry, but it's feeling so good. Going without a condom is something else. I've never done that before. Never wanted to get someone pregnant.

I feel free.

I'm also feeling entirely too much. Too much sensation, too good, too close, but I need to move.

Little by little, I start fucking Shelby, watching the way he's watching me. Watching his dick bob as I move his body. He circles his dick with his fist and shuttles it up and down. I want to do that for him, but I'm concentrating on changing the angle. Trying and experimenting until I find...

"There," he groans. "Fuck. There. Yes. Please. Do that again. Oh my god."

I repeat the move, rocking my dick in his entrance and dragging it out, wanting to pin him to the bed with my cock. I want to fucking own him.

Feelings I've never had before are absolutely taking over.

I've always been a little blasé about sex. Take it or leave it. It feels good, but it doesn't really matter who I do it with.

In this moment, Shelby owns me. I would do anything to have

him gasp the way he's doing. To have him trust me with his body this way.

To have every part of us connect—not just physically, but our hearts or spirits. To be one with him.

"You're fucking mine," I whisper, my thrusts getting harder and more erratic. Artless and somehow better.

"Yes," he hisses.

I'm floating. Flying. Feeling closer than I ever have to another human being. Feeling my body and my soul merging with his.

And I'm going to come.

I want him to come first. I slow down, fucking him more deliberately, rhythmically, making sure I get the angle right, making sure he's moaning and writhing.

Then I pull out and slap his hip. "Turn over," I order, and he scrambles to do so.

He goes up on his hands and knees, and I press down between his shoulder blades. He lowers his head willingly, and I enter him.

This time, we're really loud. He's gasping and groaning, and I'm grunting as I fuck him hard. "I'm gonna cuh-uh-ome," he wails, and his body tenses up, and he starts shaking. His head is turned to the side, and I can see the agony of pleasure on his face. I know he's coming hands-free, and that's the hottest damn thing I've ever seen.

A few more thrusts and I'm slamming up inside him, whiting out my brain, a whole-body orgasm taking over everything.

I think I fucked my brains out. And his.

I slow down, like a freight train still going down the track but coasting, until I've milked everything out of me. Inside him still, I pull him back on his knees and turn his head so our mouths can meet over his shoulder.

Our tongues collide in a hard, desperate kiss. Tired, but still wanting more of each other.

Eventually, I soften and slip out of him. There's a trail of my come running from his asshole and down his leg, and I stare at it for a moment. I run a finger through it, and he sees me doing it, then opens his mouth. I put my finger to his lips, and he sucks it so hard my dick tries to get up again.

We adjust so he's lying on his back and I'm on my side next to him. I'm not willing to stop kissing him, even though I'm out of breath.

Finally, he pulls away, and we collapse next to each other, panting. One of my hands is on my belly, going up and down with my breath. The other toys with his hair.

While I don't want to break the spell, I do anyway. "That was unbelievable," I whisper.

He turns to look at me, his eyes serious. "Yeah. It was."

CHAPTER 20

Shelby

Sex with Camden has been amazing from the start, but what we just shared was transcendent. I don't know another way to describe it.

It was *connection*. It was fucking hot. It was him taking care of me and using me in equal measure. More like he took care of me *by* using me, which is a mindfuck that I don't even want to contemplate. I'm going to be walking funny tomorrow, and I don't care at all.

Cam was supposed to be my convenient husband and maybe my friend, but he's become my boyfriend and my lover. Having a lover is something I've always wanted, and now that I know what it's like, I don't think I can go back to the kind of sex that's just a bodily function, we both get off and it's no big deal. I want him in my bed forever. I'm both sated and scared, because what the actual hell? Cam seemed *into it*. And I don't want to question that, even if I know I'm going to.

I reach out and stroke his bare arm, and he turns to me and smiles, sleepy and comfortable, then leans over to kiss me. It takes me a moment to kiss him back, because each time he does it, my brain needs to kick in. It's not automatic.

The part that's automatic is: Camden is just married to me for the health insurance. He's not actually into guys. This is him figuring out his sexuality. I am the experiment.

Except ... he said he's my boyfriend, so maybe I can allow in some hope. Maybe, like Alden says, I can not worry and create something bad in the future. After all, Cam's tongue in my mouth sure feels like something wonderful—something *more*. I pull back, and he tilts his head quizzically. "You okay?" he asks, his dark hair splayed on the white sheets.

I trace his jaw. "Yeah. I guess I didn't think you'd be so into it. I'm waiting for you to finally have a bi panic attack."

His cheeks go pink. It's frankly adorable for a tough guy to be so flustered. Then he sits up and squares his shoulders. "Not gonna happen. I like you, and I think you're hot."

"Well, I guess that's reason enough to get together with someone," I tease.

It is. I've slept with guys for only one of those reasons—or even none. But with Cam, I don't know. It just feels different. Maybe because I want to be different and to stop being played. I don't think Cam would ever play me—he's a total straight shooter. I don't think he could lie for shit even if he tried.

But that also means that if he ever hurts me, he'll do it to my face, because he's not going to pretend. In other words, I can still get rejected. And that's scary.

As if seeing all these thoughts parade through my brain, Camden tugs me to him and rolls onto his back. He's so warm under me. I like the hair on his chest and the stubble on his cheeks. I rake my hands across his pecs and tug on his nipples. He's manly and strong, and part of me wants to have someone strong take my burdens away for the first time in my life.

* * *

When I walk in from work the next day, Cam's on the phone with someone—I assume his brother—and I hear him sigh. "I'm counting the days." Pause. "Yeah, I know. I'm almost done." He looks at me and raises his eyebrows, giving me a chin-up nod.

While the logical part of me knows he's likely talking about finishing the physical therapy to fix his ankle, the scared part thinks that it's also the amount of time we have left together.

In any case, he should have the chance to choose me of his own free will, not because I moved into his house and won't leave.

That thought terrifies me—giving him the freedom he deserves. Because I'm not someone that other people want to keep around.

Before Cam can see the look on my face, I beeline out to the pool house, and ten minutes later, Cam finds me in bed, curled up into myself. A tear slides down my cheek, and I brush it away as fast as I can.

"Hey," he says, climbing onto the bed next to me. "Hey. What's going on?"

I sniffle and shake my head.

"You don't have to tell me if you don't want to, but I'll listen if you do." Cam wraps his arms around me. And oh, he feels so good.

I mutter, "I just got sad, that's all. Because I can't keep you."

Camden stiffens behind me, and his biceps flex. Then he sighs and tugs me closer. "What do you mean? Are you talking about our deal?"

"Yeah. You're almost healed up, and there's no reason you can't get your own insurance. And we're supposed to get a divorce." All of the emotions I've held in for so long come crashing out of me, and I start sobbing. Racking, messy, ugly-cry tears with snot, the kind of crying no one wants to see. "I'm just so tired of not getting what I want."

Cam kisses the top of my head. For a while, he lets me sob into his lap and doesn't say anything. Eventually, when I'm all cried out and no longer hiccuping, he asks, "What is it you want?"

"You."

He nuzzles my neck. "You have me. And I'm not letting you go, just so you know."

Oh, how I wish I could believe him. Oh, how I wish this were the way things turned out for me. "It's too good to be true."

"Why do you say that?"

I shrug. Which is hard to do when he's holding me so close.

"Not an answer," he warns.

"Cam, you're ... you've been straight. I derailed your plans. Haven't you always wanted a traditional relationship? I mean, you were going to get married to Leah. It seems pretty clear you wanted a wife, maybe kids, a nice house?"

"Have you seen my house?"

"Yeah, it's getting super cool."

Behind me, he shakes his head. "That's not what I mean. I mean, I don't need any of that." Cam stands up and hoists me up by my ass. I wrap my arms and legs around him like a koala and tuck my head against his neck.

"But what if you do?"

"I promise," he whispers, holding me close. "I honestly don't need any of those things you think I need. Don't make up a story in your head that isn't reality."

I can't help it, though, because I'm thinking about my mom. If she could throw me out like last week's leftovers, why wouldn't anyone else? I snuffle into his neck.

He walks us out—his ankle really is healed, isn't it—past the pool and back to the living room in the main house, where he sits down on the couch, taking me with him. I straddle his lap, and his hands slide up and down my back in a soothing embrace.

This guy. I still feel like crap, but also like there's something waiting for me, maybe. Like I *can* have some of the things I want.

Or maybe just the one most important thing.

I rub my nose with my sleeve. "I'm sorry I lost my shit. I get emotional sometimes."

"I think emotional support is what husbands do—or should do, anyway," he says. Then he smiles. "But you're also my boyfriend and my friend. I want to be closer to you. I wish you felt like you could confide in me. I want to be a safe place for you. I want to help you break free from the patterns of your past." He eyes me. "It's not just your mom, is it?"

I shake my head. "I don't want to give you my entire dating history unless you want to hear it, but the guys I was with were usually in one of two categories: quick hookups or ones I wanted more with. Quick hookups are no big deal. But the ones I wanted more with ended up not wanting more with me. And worse, repeatedly, I was finding guys who were either in the closet or who decided after experimenting with me that they weren't actually queer." I eye Cam. "You see how we are in the office. I'm in an environment that's safe and out and proud. I'm never going to hide who I am. And when I was with someone who made me feel like we were doing something shameful or like they couldn't be with me in public, that hurt deep, because it made me question whether all that I've fought through was a lie. Like maybe my mom was right and I shouldn't have been born." He opens his mouth to protest, and I shush him. "Yeah, I know intellectually that it's BS, but deep down, I can't help but wonder."

"They all did a number on you."

"Yes. So, I thought I was finally getting away from all of that with Evan because he was out." I make a face. "But you know how that ended."

"I wish I could say something to make it all better," Cam whispers. "But I don't know what I can do other than be here for you now."

He presses a kiss to my lips, and that gesture moves my heart even more. He's so kind, so beautiful, and he's protective of me.

This was supposed to be fake. He was supposed to be straight. I wasn't supposed to get involved.

I am very much involved.

But that doesn't stop me from kissing him back. "Being here is plenty. Thank you," I murmur. "You're the best."

"I just want you to feel good all the time."

While I want to wiggle in his lap and tell him I know a way that he can make me feel really good, in reality, I'm not thinking of sex. I'm thinking of the way I feel so protected. I've never had a protector before Cam.

"Can we watch a movie?" I ask. Because I need to relieve the tension. It's not sexual. Just, everything has been a bit too heavy, and I need a distraction from real life. I don't want to keep talking about my issues.

"Of course." He kisses me again. "What do you want to watch?"

"What's your favorite movie?" I ask.

"*A New Hope*. What's yours?" He reaches for the remote.

"Same. Can we watch it?"

"Absolutely."

Cam makes no move to get me off of his lap. Instead, he moves me so I can see the television screen while still sitting on him. He tugs a blanket from the back of the couch over us. And we watch the movie cuddled up together.

Once it's over, I reluctantly stand up, and we go down the hall and get ready for bed.

When I crawl in next to him and he wraps his arms around me, I feel so safe. Like not only will he never hurt me, but he'll make sure that no one breaks through the little bubble we have around our house. Like we are definitely going to be our own family unit.

I start kissing his bare skin because it's right here and feels so good, and he growls. "None of that. You're feeling a bit raw, I bet," he murmurs.

"We don't have to," I say. "But I wouldn't mind fooling

around a little bit if you wanted to. I know crying is cathartic, but other kinds of releases feel good, too."

"Is that what you think?"

I nod gravely.

"Then let's do it. I wouldn't want you to feel bad."

I smile as he begins to kiss his way down my body.

CHAPTER 21

Camden

One night after work, Charlie comes over for dinner, bringing pizza for all three of us. He's his usual self, meaning, although he may be a fully licensed attorney, he can still piss me the fuck off, because he's an annoying little brother.

Once we're done eating, Shelby gets up to take care of the dishes, and Charlie joins me on the couch. I feel guilty about not helping with the cleanup, especially since my ankle is almost healed, but Shelby shoos me off to go talk with my brother.

I kind of wish Charlie would leave, even though that's rude, since he did bring us a meal. But I really need some alone time with my husband. I know it's hard for him to trust people, but we've been talking more lately, and I'd hoped we were making progress.

Charlie grins. "How's it going with the husband?"

How is it going? I'm not straight. The feelings I have for Shelby have become real. I may want to not get a divorce when it's done. But Shelby may not be on the same wavelength as me. He's been hurt very deeply, and I don't know if I can do enough to help him heal.

I don't want to say any of that to my brother.

"It's fine," I say. "He's good."

Charlie looks at me. "Fine? Good? That's very informative. You're almost done with your whole no-weight-on-your-foot thing. Are you excited about wrapping up the temporary marriage and getting back into the dating world? Or are you two already seeing people anyhow?"

"Don't you have to get home? Or go somewhere?" I ask.

"Nope. I wanna hang with my big brother." Charlie settles in, cracking open another beer, and I want to groan.

But Shelby, sweetheart that he is, comes in from the kitchen with a smile and opens one for himself, too, sitting next to me on the couch.

"Hey," Charlie says. "A bunch of us from the office are going to go skiing over Thanksgiving, since there's early snow. Noah and August, Sam and Jules, Alden and Danny, Reyna, Demi. Want to go? Both of you, of course."

I glance down at my ankle. "If I'm careful, I think I can handle a bunny slope. Do you ski, Shelby?"

Shelby shrugs. "Um, I have. I'm not that great at it. But I like the warm drinks afterward."

"I'll send you the info where we're all staying," Charlie says.

"Do you want to go?" Shelby and I ask each other at the same time.

We both laugh. "Sure," we say at the same time and laugh again.

Charlie shakes his head. "You two are something else. The plan is to go to Sam and Jules's beach house for Blackest Friday, then skiing for the weekend."

"Blackest Friday?" I ask.

He shrugs. "It's a thing that he came up with this year, apparently, and Sam said we could all come. Guess that's the advantage of living in California—you can go from the snow to the beach in a day. Or vice versa."

Shelby and I exchange looks. "Okay, we're in. What do we have to do?" he says.

"Just bring something from the past that you want to burn."

I frown. "What the hell?"

"Jules said that, instead of supporting the capitalistic economy for Black Friday, they're going to have Blackest Friday. He's going to play death metal music, have a bonfire, and burn all the things from our past that we want to let go of."

Shelby looks impressed. "Okay. We can do that. What do you think, Cam? Want to get rid of something from your past?"

"Bring something symbolic that I want to burn?" I ask.

"Yeah, I dunno. Crap from Leah. Your medical bills. Shit like that."

"I'm in. What are you going to burn?" I ask Charlie.

"A motion for summary judgment I lost."

That makes me roll my eyes. "Of course. What about you, Shelby?"

"I'll have to think about it," he says, sipping his beer.

I can think of a few things that would be appropriate for him to let go of. But that's for him to decide. Charlie still makes no move to leave, and I have a random thought about burning *him* in effigy.

"What have you been working on lately?" Charlie says. "Any new projects we should film?"

"We're finally getting to the kitchen," I say, deciding I should join the crowd and opening a beer for myself.

Even though what I really want is to get my husband alone and ... get him naked. I don't feel like I can share that with Charlie, though.

Why am I so hesitant to come out to my brother? He came out to me.

He later told me he'd nearly hurled before he said the words, too. And now I understand how he felt, because even though I know he loves me and he'll support me, it'll still change our relationship. Change ... is the unknown. Which is scary.

Well, that's something. Here I am having a normal conversation with my brother and my husband, and inside, I'm having an existential crisis.

"That's cool," Charlie says. "Want to work up a schedule so we can film? I can make sure to come by."

"I love watching you two work together," Shelby says warmly.

"Okay," I say.

Charlie tilts his head at me.

"What?" I ask, feeling defensive. I cross my arms over my chest.

"You seem a little off. If you don't want to do it, we don't have to. Just, your videos with me get a lot of views, and a lot of views is fun."

"No, we can do it. I'm good with it."

Now it's Charlie's turn to cross his arms. "Yeaaah," he says slowly. "Okay." He narrows his eyes.

He'll win, and we both know it, so I might as well tell him. If my gay brother isn't the safest person besides my husband to come out to, I'm not sure who is.

"I think I'm bisexual," I blurt.

Charlie stares. He frowns. Then his face eases into a slow smile. "No. *Way*. Wait," he says, starting to get excited. "You and Shelby?"

"Yeah, I like my husband for real. We're dating now. Go figure."

Charlie stands up and comes over to me, takes the beer from my hand and sets it down, tugs me up off the couch, and engulfs me in a hug.

He doesn't say anything else, and somehow, that says more than anything. A lump forms in my throat. I hadn't realized that by holding this in, by holding part of me back from him, I'd been missing out on some massive support.

When we break apart, I glance over at Shelby, and he's wiping his eyes.

I sit back down next to Shelby and pull him into my lap. "I

guess I can quit pretending with you," I tell Charlie. I kiss Shelby on the neck, and he squirms against me.

Charlie grins. "I'm seriously happy for you two. That's awesome."

I wrap my arms around Shelby tighter, and Charlie goes to open another beer, then thinks twice about it and hands it to me.

"I'll let you two be. By the way, Mom told me she wants you to come over for a barbecue. I've been putting her off, thinking that you were just married for the insurance, but I guess I'll tell her you're good to go."

I don't want to explain anything to anyone, but if I know my mom, she's chomping at the bit to have a party. "If she keeps it small, that would be fine," I say, "if Shelby is okay with it."

"Yeah, it's okay," Shelby says.

Charlie claps each of us on the shoulder. "Congratulations, guys. And I get it, Cam. Why you needed a bit to sort it out. If you ever want to talk, I'll listen."

My asshole of a brother is being so much less of an ass than usual. But I've always known that was a front. He's just misunderstood.

Charlie closes the door behind him, and Shelby exclaims, "I can't believe you came out!"

I kiss his eyelids. "It's funny, right? I mean, I married you, but everyone close to me knew that it was a ruse. Except, turns out, it isn't anymore." I swallow hard. "I want to prove to you that I'm not like the other guys you've dated."

"You definitely aren't."

* * *

My parents have us over for a celebratory barbecue the following weekend. Charlie and Reyna cook. Reyna's brought her best friend from college, Max, who is out visiting. He's small, like Shelby, and I can see Charlie eyeing him. But then Max starts talking about some firefighters in Vermont, and Charlie backs away.

Mom pulls out the photo albums, which have too many shots of me and Leah in them. I don't want to hide my past from Shelby, but I also don't want him thinking that I miss her. I don't. When he makes it through them, commenting on how nicely my mom laid out her scrapbooks, he gets up and starts looking at all the family photographs on the walls. "Yeah, they liked to take pictures of the three of us," I say, laughing at one where we're surrounded by pumpkins. "God, that's embarrassing."

I want to be careful, though. I imagine his mom didn't put up photos like this. He certainly didn't have the same kind of upbringing we did.

But he doesn't seem to mind. "I love these!" Shelby says. He points to one where I'm playing with a set of Lincoln Logs. "You liked them, too?"

I nod. "No surprise that I ended up a contractor. I always liked building things. Creating something from nothing, you know?"

"I do. It's why I like making crafts like vision boards. Or hug books."

I give him a puzzled look. "What's that?"

"We have a client who needed a hug, but I wasn't going to be there to give it to him. So I made him a book of hugs from the internet. I cut out all these pictures of kittens hugging and T-rexes trying to hug, that sort of thing."

"That's cute. Was the client a little old lady?"

He chuckles. "No. A porn star."

I do a double take.

"Porn stars need love, too, and he's been having a tough time of it. Anyway, all I wanted to say was that I get it. I understand why you like building things. I do it, too, just with paper and pictures."

"Yeah."

He looks at another picture where I'm sitting on top of the doghouse. "You on a roof? Not surprising."

"Guess it started early," I say. "Hang on. Let me show you where I used to go once I got a little bit older."

"Not the doghouse?"

"Not the doghouse," I assure him.

We go upstairs, where I pull a ladder down from the ceiling. I climb up into the attic, trying to mostly put weight on my good foot, and Shelby follows. Once we're up there, I open the window, remove the screen, and we crawl out onto the roof. The lights of Los Angeles twinkle around us, and a cool breeze plays across our faces.

"Oh, wow," Shelby says. "I love it up here."

"I do, too. I used to come up here when my siblings were being too noisy." There's noise outside, of course—traffic, a plane, laughter from the house across the street. But I feel removed from it all. "Come here," I say, and Shelby crawls into my lap. "Thanks for coming tonight," I murmur. "You made my mom happy."

"Did I?"

"Uh-huh. Me, too."

We sit out there, just watching the world. After a moment Shelby says quietly, "Reyna told me you'd intended to rent out the pool house as an Airbnb. Now that we're ... I mean, I could move my stuff out of there and free it up for you if you want."

I shake my head. "No. I don't want strangers coming in right now."

Shelby bites his lip. "You were so stressed about money before, and I don't want to prevent you from getting out of debt."

"Life seemed pretty dire there for a while," I admit. "With not knowing how bad my foot might be, and no way of working." I shrug. "Having health insurance makes a huge difference, anxiety-wise, and I guess with perspective, I've calmed down some. Leah sent over a check to pay for some of the costs from the wedding, and I'll maybe refinance the house, since its value has gone up. Do some debt consolidation. I was panicking before, but now that I know not everything is due today, it seems more manageable."

"Good. And I can contribute more in terms of rent."

"Not necessary. But I appreciate the offer."

"Then I'll keep the offer open." He turns, and I kiss him. He tastes like beer and barbecued chicken and something familiar and homey. It feels like Shelby and I have been together our whole lives, not just the past few months. He should be my companion in everything I do for the rest of my life.

Maybe I was waiting to be with him. He opened me up to see other possibilities. Maybe he's my soulmate.

I suck in a breath, and he gazes at me. "What's up?" Shelby asks.

"Nothing."

Is Shelby my soulmate?

With how he always seems to know what I need even before I do, I kind of think he is. It's not that he finishes my sentences or things like that, but, dammit, I'm starting to have strong feelings for the guy, and I'm not wanting this thing to end whenever we're supposed to be ending it.

... so maybe we don't.

How revolutionary would that be? To stay married to my husband because I genuinely want to be married to him?

CHAPTER 22

Shelby

"Happy three-month anniversary!" Alden says, beaming as he leans against the reception desk.

"Thanks," I say, sounding a little glum. I'm in a mood, and to distract myself, I'm working on a project for Cam—everyone is so used to me having craft supplies out at the reception desk that no one asks me what I'm doing, and I'm caught up on my other work—but I don't know if I'll ever have the chance to give it to him.

Alden frowns. "Why don't you sound happy?"

"Because ... his ankle is pretty much healed, and soon it's going to be the test of whether we stay together or split up." I blow out a breath, ruffling my bangs.

Alden's eyes widen. "You're not going to split up anymore. Are you? Just because that was the original plan doesn't mean that you have to do it," he scolds.

"I guess."

"No," he says forcefully. "You know it's true. Is he someone you'd want to stay with?"

Nodding, I say, "Yeah."

He beams. "That's wonderful!"

"No, it's not." I kick at my chair legs.

"Why not?" Alden cocks his head, looking genuinely curious.

I groan, and I know it comes out whiny. But I'm allowed to whine, at least a little bit, aren't I? "Nothing is going the way it was supposed to. For starters, this was supposed to be easy, and he was supposed to be straight." I pick up a pen and start doodling on a scratch pad, needing to do *something*.

Alden shifts his weight. "So, what's the problem? He's not as straight as he thought, you like him more than you expected to ... I'm not seeing how this is bad."

"Ugh," I say. "I do like him. He's sweet, and kind, and I want him."

"And he's handsome and your husband, and he wants you. That's great!"

My voice drops to a harsh whisper as Demi walks by. "I wasn't supposed to let pesky feelings get involved. I mean, Cam was supposed to be untouchable. Not literally. Just, you know, he wasn't supposed to be an option."

"But he's so comfortable in his sexuality that he's okay with being a little bit bi."

"Or a lot bi, apparently." I sigh. "He even came out to his brother. He's really, really good in bed, and I have no idea how I happened to get so lucky. Except it's terrible luck, because this amazing guy happens to be the one I'm married to."

"That makes zero sense. You're talking in circles."

"It's because I don't understand how to deal with this. I don't know what the right thing to do is: to stick with our agreement or to follow my feelings."

"Feelings, obviously."

"Don't say that so fast. I don't know what I'm doing, and I don't know if I can handle being with him for real. I've never had a good boyfriend. He says I have an issue with thinking I don't deserve nice things. Or things at all."

"He's right," Alden says. "So … he's one of those nice things that you don't think you deserve?"

"Yeah. That." I stare down at my desk.

Alden reaches over and squeezes my hand. "Just so you know … you're wrong, Shelby. You deserve to be happy. Just talk with him some more."

* * *

So I do.

When I get home from work, I curl up next to Cam on the couch. He's watching football, and he wraps an arm around me and kisses the top of my head. He's so readily affectionate, it throws me for a loop. I'm like a mangy cat, unused to getting affection or any positive attention, while he's a happy dog.

"Cam," I say, when there's a commercial break. He mutes the TV and turns to me.

"Yeah?"

"Can we talk about something?"

A distressed look flashes across his face, probably due to my tone of voice. "Sure," he says warily.

"It's not something bad."

"Okay." I can't miss the relief in how his shoulders relax.

I straighten my backbone and look at him straight in the eyes. "It's just … I like you. A lot."

"I like you, too." He smiles. Ugh. That smile. But it fades when he sees my expression.

"No, that's the problem, Camden. When this started, you were safe—I mean, I was safe with you—because you were straight. Someone I didn't have any issues with, because nothing was ever going to happen between us."

"You don't want us to—" Cam goes to move, and I quickly straddle him, cupping his stubbled jaw.

"No. I do. You don't understand." I sigh. "Probably because

I'm not explaining this clearly." I start again. "I've always liked you. I had a crush on you before you even talked to me the first time." He raises an eyebrow, but I keep going. "At firm events, and, um, on your videos, I always thought you were hot and kind. I always wanted you, but I also knew you were off-limits, which meant that you were safe to fantasize about, since nothing would ever happen. I didn't have to risk getting my heart involved. Now, because we've been doing this"—I gesture at our bodies—"it's not safe anymore."

Cam shifts under me. "Then we should stop. I'd never want you to feel bad."

"That's not what I'm saying. I don't want to feel the way I do, and yet I don't want to stop. I like you, Cam. I really do." I catch his eyes, and they look so sincere. I force myself to keep going. "But if you're not in this with me for real, if it's just a temporary thing ... I mean, it always was supposed to be, that was the deal, but things have changed. I guess what I'm saying is, if I'm going to get dumped at the end of this because you're not on the same page, I think I want to know now." My hands are shaking, and I feel light-headed and nauseated. I don't want to pressure him, but I also don't want him to say no.

"Oh, Shelby," he says. His gentle tone reaches somewhere deep inside me. "You just need someone to love you."

"I do," I whisper. "I don't know if that someone is you."

He shrugs. "I don't know if it is, either, but I feel like it is. Don't you?"

"Yeah. That's what scares me so much."

"I don't want you to be scared. Is that what's been bothering you? That you don't think I truly like you, deep down, regardless of health insurance or anything else?"

I nod, picking at his shirt.

"Shelby, let me say this clearly: I really care about you. What we have together is real. If you ever start doubting us, tell me, and I'll remind you." He looks thoughtful. "My parents have a good marriage, and they've shown us how they do it: by being there. I want to be there for you. And I will be there."

His words make me warm inside, and they feel both safe and dangerous at the same time. He's giving me what I want, but I can't help knowing that it could be taken away. He could be doing this just to humor me. Except I think he's not.

Somehow, what he just said seems like more of a vow than the one we made at the courthouse. With no witnesses, no paperwork, no legal issues. Declaring something to each other. Is that what marriage is?

"Cam? This unconditional support that you're offering ... I've never had that. Support has always been dependent on what I could give back. Or, with my mom, how much I could stay invisible and out of the way."

He gives me a sad smile. "Then I'll keep at it and keep showing you that I want to be with you."

"Thanks," I whisper. "I'm sorry I'm a work in progress."

"We all are."

I cuddle into him, but somewhere inside me is the little boy who wasn't wanted. And he'll always worry that promises won't mean anything in the end.

I can't help but be hopeful, though. As Alden says, just because something happened before doesn't mean I'm doomed to repeat it. I can move past the past and into the future. Or, better, the present. Because right now, I have my beautiful husband—and boyfriend—under me, and he's looking pretty damned wonderful.

"So, what's this about you having a crush on me before you really knew me?" Cam's tone is gentle but teasing.

"I thought you were unbelievably gorgeous, but it was more than your looks. I loved how you supported your siblings. Showing up with them to events and, I don't know. It just felt like the love you have for your brother and sister was unconditional."

"That's because it is. Always has been and always will be." He pushes my shoulder. "Still ... I'm not fishing for a compliment, but you don't usually get a crush on someone you don't know because of their insides, do you?"

"I absolutely did. I watched so many of your videos, and while you didn't always talk in them"—many are time-lapse with a music overlay—"you showed courtesy to your brother, even when you were teasing him. And you'd move seamlessly when putting something heavy in place in your backyard or holding things for each other. You worked so well together."

"We do."

"It's special, is all I'm saying. And that translated through the screen. Like, you joked with each other, but I could also tell that you were, I don't know. Protective of him."

He looks to the side. "And now that you know me, what do you think? Do I match up to the crush?"

"Oh my god, Camden, you go so much beyond. Everything that you hinted at—or that I inferred—is true. You really are loving and generous and supportive."

"Thanks. But that's not exactly what I meant. It's more ... Okay, even if I haven't been totally different than who you thought I was, I don't know. There are still things about me that might annoy you. Like my taste in movies or the way I eat spaghetti or how I leave my boots by the front door or something."

"Why would leaving your boots by the front door bother anyone? It means you're thoughtful enough not to track dirt around the house."

"Bad example. You know what I mean."

I nod and wrap my arms around his waist. "We like the same movies, and I don't think you eat spaghetti weird. I guess the things I've learned—that you have a weakness for fix-it reality shows and RVs, you eat pretty much everything and don't have a belly, you're stubborn and prideful but also loyal—all of that makes you even more attractive."

"For what it's worth, I feel the same way. I mean, about liking your insides now that I've gotten to know you. Before, I saw this striking man with great hair who worked with my siblings. Who always caught my eye. And now I can truly see how great you are inside. You take care of people. Take care of things. You get shit done, Shelby. Speaking as a contractor who builds things for a living, seeing someone do that is hot."

"Thanks," I say. Then I voice something I've been wondering about. "You told your brother that you're bi. Do you think, now that we've been together for a while, that you're attracted to men in general, or is it just me?"

I'm not sure which answer I'd prefer, but for some reason, it makes me nervous to ask.

"I don't know."

"But you always thought you were straight. Before."

"I had a steady girlfriend for a long time, and there was no reason to question it. I think on the sexuality spectrum I still skew more toward straight. I don't find that I'm attracted to many more guys than you. I guess I feel like I don't need to figure that out. You're enough for me."

I blink. "Being enough for someone is quite possibly the nicest compliment someone has ever given me."

He grins, and we don't end up seeing any more of the football game. I'm good with that.

Cam twists us so he's hovering over me, and he very, very slowly rubs his fabric-covered cock against mine. We both groan. I grab his ass, and he kisses me deep, and I say, "This is my new favorite way to watch TV."

He smiles against my lips, and his hands start exploring. He traces across my forehead and down my cheeks, then continues farther down. His movements are slow, but our kisses are fucking hot.

Deep. Lots of tongue. Meaning it.

After how emotionally vulnerable I let myself be with him, I'm needing to express what I feel for him in some way other than words. I want that communion with him again. He breaks away, tugging at the waist of my shorts. I raise my hips and help him get me naked, and now I'm sprawled out on the couch, my cock erect, my hair flopping against the pillow. He shoves his boxers down and kisses my collarbone, then grasps my cock with his hand.

"You're absolutely gorgeous, babe. Inside and out. I want you in every way. Can I show you at least one way?" Cam asks.

I know in the past I've confused sex and feelings. But this is sex *with* feelings.

"Yes," I gasp. "Fuck. Yes."

He gives it a slow stroke, then kisses me some more. "Wanna get the lube?"

"Yeah." I wriggle out from under him and grab it from the bedroom, returning as fast as I can, and he squirts some into his hand. Meanwhile, I'm trying to I-spy his cock, and I'm rewarded when he sits back on his heels.

My husband is gorgeous all over.

Later, when I'm curled next to him, sated and happy, I trace up and down his arm and wonder how I got so lucky. It feels like a chance occurrence, but I don't think it was. Something or someone put us together. And I want to stay with him.

* * *

We spend Thanksgiving at Cam's parents' house with the rest of his family, and the next evening we're on the beach in Malibu, holding warm drinks provided by Julian Hill's personal chef, who magicked them out of nowhere. Jules had a stack of blankets waiting, and we're all bundled up around a massive bonfire.

"Is everyone ready to burn cursed objects?" Jules asks, the flames licking behind him so we can barely make out his expression.

His accent is really hot. I mean, Cam is the hottest, but I can appreciate Jules's voice.

"I can't wait to see," Sam says. "Did everyone bring something from their past that they want to get rid of? Who's going first?"

Danny steps forward with a small box in his hand, holding it out for everyone to see. "This is the ring I was going to give my high school boyfriend. He dumped me on prom night."

There's a collective gasp. Alden smiles at him, then reaches over and squeezes his hand.

Danny scoffs. "I've moved past it, clearly, and at this point I look at this thing with a little fondness. Like, okay, past me. That was you as a puppy, and now you're a real dog."

"A junkyard dog," Charlie says.

"A hunk of a dog," Alden whispers.

"At any rate, this is the final nail in the coffin," Danny says.

"Throw it, mate," Jules says, an arm wrapped around Sam.

Danny does. I wonder if the ring will melt or if it will still be there in the morning. I suppose it doesn't matter. It's going back to the earth. We all watch the fire, and Jules claps his hands. "Who's next?"

Sam takes a piece of paper out of his pocket and stands up. "This is the first speech my grandfather's speechwriter wrote for me. It was the first stop on my way to not being myself."

"You still had a copy?" Jules asks.

"No," Sam admits. "I had to look back in my email and print it out, but it wasn't hard to find. Everything is there. At any rate, I'm getting free from my past. I'm claiming my own story, not one that someone makes up for me." He tosses the page into the bonfire. We all clap, and Jules whoops and pulls him in for a kiss.

Danny whistles. "Okay, next?"

Noah steps forward, brandishing a piece of paper. "These are the discharge instructions from the hospital when I fell off my bike."

"The time I proposed?" August asks.

Noah nods. "Yeah, the first time I turned you down."

"I don't think that's a bad memory," August says. "I mean," he adds quickly, when everyone stares at him in horror, "obviously the love of my life being hurt was awful, but it was the catalyst that made me change so that I could see our relationship for real and figure out what you really meant to me."

"Well, now I don't want to burn it," Noah says, taking a step back and crossing his arms over his chest.

"I think you should. Take the risk," August murmurs.

Noah grins and tosses it in.

"What about you?" I ask Cam. "Is there something from your past that you want to burn? Some cursed object?"

He holds out a box. "These are the leftover invitations from my wedding with my ex-girlfriend, the bills from the wedding, and my final medical bill for rehabbing my ankle. I'm leaving all that crap in the past." He shakes his foot. "I'm fully cleared for skiing this weekend."

We get a round of applause, but I feel funny.

Now I'm going to find out if he really does want to stay with me. If his words were empty promises or something I can trust.

I want to trust him. I need to move past this pain.

"Those were the things from my past that don't serve me anymore," Cam says as he adds them to the bonfire. "Babe, do you have something you want to toss?"

I swallow hard and hold up the birthday card I've carted around for years. "This."

Cam does a sharp intake. "Wow."

"Do I have to explain it?" I whisper, looking around at the group. They're all familiar, friendly faces. Ones I know wouldn't judge me. But still, it's hard to tell the story of my mother's rejection.

"No," Sam says gently.

I walk up to the fire, holding the card. It's worn from my opening and closing it so many times. Taking it from shitty apartment to shitty apartment. Then to decent ones. And finally to where I am now, with Cam.

I want to throw off my past expectations. I want to throw off feeling like I wasn't enough. I want to lose the dead weight.

I don't know if I can do that. But at least I can stop carrying around a reminder that I wasn't enough for my mom.

With watering eyes—I'm sure it's from the smoke—I toss the card into the bonfire and watch the flames lick at it until it disintegrates and the black ash rises into the night.

And then I begin to tell my friends what happened to me. They listen, some of them wincing, as I tell them how my mom took care of me for eighteen years and not a day more. When I'm done, Cam gathers me in his arms and holds me tight. My friends all murmur appreciation that I told them.

Jules picks up his phone, cranks up the death metal, and we sit by the fire, watching the past burn.

CHAPTER 23

Camden

I t's cold on the mountain, the brisk air and bright sun working together to let us to see for miles. Up here in the trees and snow, it's hard to believe in the smog of Los Angeles.

I've finally been released—mostly—from the doctors and physical therapists, but I'm going to baby my ankle. I wrapped it up and braced it, and I'm planning on sticking to the bunny slopes. At worst (best?), Shelby and I can enjoy après-ski drinks by the fire in the lodge.

I thought about snowboarding, but I feel like going old school. Shelby's with me, his platinum hair sticking out under the bright pink glasses that are perched atop his head. He looks like he's from the eighties, and I dig it.

"Ready?" I ask, as we start trudging to the lift.

"Absolutely."

Noah and August are behind us. "Those two are such daredevils sometimes," Shelby says. "You'd never know it by the way they look." He sighs. "At least they finally got their heads out of their asses enough to realize that they've been totally in love with each other ever since they met."

I scoff. "Haven't they known each other since they were kids?"

"Yep." He grins. "And Noah's been heart-eyes for August that whole time. Like August said last night, he only realized it when Noah got hurt going down a mountain too fast on a bike—but it was always there."

"You know talking about that kind of injury isn't the best thing to do right before hopping on a ski lift?"

"I know. Still."

We reach the lift and position ourselves to sit on the bench as it takes us up.

"This always nerves me out a little bit," Shelby says, his legs swinging. "Being up so high with nothing around and nothing really holding us in."

"You have to trust that you're not going to do anything foolish."

"Are you going to do anything foolish?" he asks.

I lean over and kiss him and hear a catcall from behind us. It must be August. "Does that count?"

"Nope." His eyes twinkle. "I do like how you're so comfortable with PDA."

I shrug. "I've always liked how you taste. From the moment we were married."

He giggles. "Awesome." Then he sighs dreamily. "That first kiss was amazing, I have to say."

"It's nice that we have some memories now, when we didn't even know each other back then."

Shelby moves so he's more snuggled into me, and I wrap an arm around him. It's awkward, given our poles and the puffy jackets, but we manage. Eventually, the top comes into sight, and we tilt up our skis to dismount the lift.

I look at the choice of ski runs. "Will you think less of me if we don't do the black diamond course? I still want to be careful with my ankle."

"I'd never think less of you for not doing something rash.

Besides, I told you I'm not the best skier anyway." He smiles and points to an intermediate run. "Let's take this one."

"Sounds good." We take off down the mountain, the cold wind rushing against our faces, feeling like our bodies are being propelled down the hill by more than gravity. We whiz past evergreen trees, enjoying the scenery and the clean air. Even though I'm taking it easy on my ankle, I'm giddy with the pleasure of getting outdoors and stretching myself this way. And the fact that I'm with Shelby makes it that much better.

When we get to a midpoint that levels out, we stop for a moment to catch our breath. "I can tell my thighs are getting more of a workout than usual," Shelby says.

I smirk at him. "I can work out your thighs in a number of ways."

He shivers, but I assume it's not from the cold. "Yes, please."

When we make it to the bottom of the hill, we're both grinning. From the exhilaration of the way it feels to zip down the mountain, yes. But also because I feel closer to him than I've felt with anyone. Ever.

After a few more runs, we take a break for lunch. We deposit our gear on a rack, then clomp inside in our snow boots, where we end up ordering hot pizza and cold beer and sitting by a roaring fire. Eventually, our friends join us, but it still feels intimate.

Everyone is starting to couple off. Noah and August. Alden and Danny. Even my sister is dating someone. Charlie doesn't have a date with him, but he's prickly, so that doesn't surprise me.

"Are you two going to stay together?" Alden asks. Then he stiffens, remembering that he's one of the few who knows the entire story about why Shelby and I got married.

"Absolutely. He's it for me," I say.

Shelby gives me a weird look. I think he's trying to figure out how to cover Alden's faux pas and also how to react to what I just said.

I lean over and whisper in his ear, "I mean it."

He swallows hard and nods. "That's amazing."

"Are you two going to ski some more or go back to the cabin?" Danny asks.

"While I'd usually want to ski more, I don't want to put too much strain on my leg," I say.

"Uh-huh," August says. "If you guys need alone time, just tell us."

"We need alone time," Shelby says, and everyone laughs.

"I can't argue with that," I say.

They all laugh and shoo us out. After ditching our ski gear on the porch of our cabin, we go inside, where it's warm and welcoming, and we shed our outer layers quickly, in between kisses. God knows I want this man.

We strip each other out of shirts and pants, then take off our underclothes, leaving them in a trail to the bedroom. I'm so glad we got our own cabin. We definitely need privacy.

When we get to the bedroom, Shelby grins. "Let's go in the hot tub first."

"Sounds good to me."

"Naked."

"I'm scandalized," I say dryly. But I'm not. We have a private hot tub on the back deck, and it's only visible from the house. We grab towels and go outside. While the air is cold, the tub is steaming when we take the cover off, and we slide in.

"Ahhh," we say simultaneously.

After we get settled, I tug him to me, and he straddles my lap easily, toying with my piercings. He never seems to get tired of playing with them, and I'm certainly not complaining. Then he wraps his arms around me and kisses me. With his tongue in my mouth and his dick rubbing against me, I drift into a hazy space of pleasure. The hot water feels so good, and Shelby's a balm for my soul.

There's something so sexy about the way he gives back as

much as he takes. How our kisses turn into battles that we both win.

"I wonder if I could fuck you in a hot tub," I muse. "Would you like that?"

He nods. "I can get some lube." He scrambles out of the tub and disappears into the cabin without bothering to dry off.

I have no idea if this will work, but when he comes back, I massage his ass as he writhes on top of me, and eventually he lets me play with his hole. While I loosen him up, he's sucking on my neck, my earlobes. We're kissing and rubbing against each other, and fuck, why didn't I get myself a husband before? Though I know the important part isn't "a husband." It's Shelby. He turns me on more than anyone I've ever been with before.

Once he's loose, I say, "I'm going to fuck you bent over the side. That work for you?" Our skin is so heated from the water that it doesn't matter what kind of frigid air we're dealing with.

He nods, and I haul us partway out of the tub. Then I lube myself up and spear him on my dick. He groans in pleasure just as loudly as I do. I love this. I love fucking him. I love how his tight heat feels around my bare cock.

I love that we trust each other enough to go bare.

I love that, in this sloppy fuck, we're doing more than getting each other off. We're connecting. We're making love.

Yeah, this isn't just a fuck. I'm making love to my husband.

As he twists around to kiss me over his shoulder, I think he knows it.

And we're going to keep doing this as long as we can.

CHAPTER 24

Shelby

Camden and I return from the ski weekend, and I look around his house. When I got here a few months ago, the place was a disaster: bare studs, no flooring, hardly any lighting.

Now, it's finished, with freshly painted walls, new flooring, shiny fixtures in the kitchen, and even new furniture in most of the rooms. We've hung photos and paintings, and the place is a real, cozy home.

A home where I'm not totally sure I belong—even though I want to. Now that it's all fixed up for him, he's all set. Moreover, he's healed. Cam's returned to work full-time, and he insists on cooking dinner, doing the dishes, taking care of the things I did when he was laid up. I don't know that he needs me around anymore.

There's a file folder in my messenger bag with printouts from insurance companies that are ready to enroll a small business owner like Camden, especially since he doesn't have a preexisting condition anymore.

And there's another file folder with rooms to rent in Los Angeles. I've found a place quickly before. I can do it again.

I listened when Cam said that he wants me to stay—but how do I know for sure unless we keep to our agreement? If we actually get the divorce and he still wants me after that ... then I'll believe him.

So while I listen to my husband's quiet breathing in the middle of the night, I stare at the ceiling and wonder what I should do next.

* * *

On Monday morning, I walk into Sam's office.

"Hey," he says, looking up with a smile. "Wasn't this weekend fun?"

I nod. "Yeah. Sure." I swallow hard.

Sam studies me. "What's up? Is something wrong?"

"I need a recommendation. Do you know who here can handle a divorce?"

"Reyna. She's the best family law attorney we have."

I shake my head. "No, that won't work."

Sam frowns. "Why not?"

"Because it's about her brother."

He scrunches up his face. "Charlie? Why does Charlie ..." He pauses, and if this weren't Sam Stone, who's always in control of himself, I think his mouth might fall open a little. "Camden? Don't tell me *you're* getting a divorce."

My chest constricts. "I think I have to."

"What do you mean?"

"Cam and I have an arrangement. We agreed to get married for a few months, until he healed and got health insurance and I found a new place to stay. And we've done that."

"I'm confused. That's why you got married?"

I nod, miserable.

"You guys seemed really close up on the mountain. And at Jules's house. It didn't seem like an ... arrangement."

"Oh, I'm completely in love with him," I admit. There's no point in pretending otherwise.

"But you think he doesn't share your feelings?"

I think about what Cam has told me. The way he holds me. The way he fixes me dinner and gives me rides places, even when I could drive myself. The way he smiles when I tell him things. The way we make crafts together. The way I help him with his projects and make him laugh. The way he feels inside me.

The way we have private jokes about too much sweet-and-sour sauce on egg rolls and advice-slash-affirmation cookies and galactic OSHA IIPPs and Venn diagrams. I swallow.

Sam nods. "Uh-huh. That's what I thought. You're scared to ask."

"Sure. Because what if the answer is 'No, I don't love you back'? I've had enough people tell me that in my life. I don't need one more."

"Oh, Shelby." Sam stands up, comes over, and rubs my shoulder, and while the sympathy is nice, it doesn't feel as good as Cam's touch would.

I sigh.

"I think you know the right answer here," he says. "You should talk with him."

"What if things go all to hell?"

"Divorcing a man you're in love with isn't exactly ideal."

"Yeah. I guess I just wish I could stick my head in the sand. Why do things always go bad, even when they start out so good?"

Sam grins and shakes his head. "They don't. Things can just keep getting better and better."

I snort. "That sounds like Pollyanna. Or Alden Meyer."

"I didn't take you for a cynic, Shelbs. I think as a society, we have a tendency to plan for the worst rather than hope for the best. To worry that things will go wrong. But many times, there's an equal probability that they won't, and we've worried for nothing."

"Yeah, that's exactly what Alden says. And I wish I could believe you both."

"Maybe you could try. And maybe it will work out. Don't self-sabotage." Sam gives me a sad smile. "But if at the end of the day you need divorce papers, I'll help. I'll be here for you, whatever you need." He clicks a few times on the computer. "I'll send you a link to the self-help website where you can fill out the forms."

* * *

I get home before Cam does, and I lie on the couch, staring at the ceiling and watching the fan go around and around.

I don't know what I was thinking, falling in love with Cam. Clearly, I *wasn't* thinking. I was letting my foolish heart take charge, and that is not the way to happiness, judging by how it's never worked for me in the past.

Camden walks in from work, his backward baseball cap holding in his curls, his jeans dirty from the job.

"Hey, babe," he says, coming over and kissing me. "I need to shower and then—" He stops, catching the look on my face. He sits down on the coffee table and starts taking off his boots. "Hey," he says quietly. "What's wrong?"

I sit up and hand him a manila envelope.

He takes it but doesn't go to open it. "What's this?"

"I talked to the insurance broker for our office, and she can get you a quote for insurance for your business. If you band together with a few other GCs, it's even more affordable."

Camden's expression is very strange. I thought he'd be glad to know that insurance can be affordable, but he's not looking totally happy. More ... conflicted? "Okay. Thanks."

"And I've found a few places where I can move."

"*What?*"

I haven't, actually. Sam and I talked some more this afternoon, and he said I could stay in his old condo until I find another place, since he's moved in with Jules.

"And there's a divorce petition in there."

Cam blinks at me, startled, and his expression turns to one of pain. I've hurt him, and I hate that. But one of us has to take the initiative here.

How else will I ever find out if this thing between us is real?

I hold out another envelope. "I can't serve you with the papers, but if you want to get a divorce, we can sign this stipulation. I can get it filed, and you'll be done. I mean, we have to wait six months for it to be final, but that's just a technicality."

He stares at me and doesn't move for a long time. Finally, he reaches out and takes the envelope. "Is this what you want?" he asks.

No! I want to scream. *No! I want you. I want to be with you for the rest of my days.*

"It doesn't matter what I want," I mutter, unable to lie to him.

"What do you mean, it doesn't matter? You matter, Shelby."

"I want to follow through on what we agreed to. That's all."

He scrubs his face in exasperation. "*Why*?"

"Because it's better than waiting around for you to do it. People don't stay with me, Cam. They leave."

"I don't want to leave you!" he almost yells. "And I don't want you to leave me," he continues in a quieter tone. "Unless you don't want to be with me."

I wring my hands. "What are we supposed to do, then?"

"Are you doing this simply because that's what we agreed at the beginning?"

I nod.

"I've contemplated breaking another bone just to have an excuse to keep you around longer," he says.

"That's ridiculous."

"It's no more ridiculous than you thinking we have to get a

divorce because we got married under circumstances that have now changed."

I blink at him, tears forming. "What are you saying?"

"I don't know how to make it any clearer. I'm not going to leave you just because I have insurance. Or because my ankle is healed."

I want to believe him. I want to, so much. And my brain does, I think. Logically, I know Cam isn't a liar. He wouldn't say this if he didn't mean it. But my heart can't make sense of his words. People don't stay.

Cam shakes his head. "No. I'm not signing a stipulation." He falters. "Not unless that's what you want."

I groan. "I don't know what I want."

"Then don't be so hasty. Can we talk about this some more?"

"What else is there to talk about?"

"How about that if neither one of us wants this to end, it doesn't have to."

"But how will I know this is truly what you want," I whisper, "unless you choose me?"

"Don't you know that I'll choose you every time?"

"No." I shake my head. "I don't think I know that."

He sighs. "Then let me figure out how to prove it to you."

I look him straight in the eyes. "I know I'm an impossible pain in the ass. I was a burden to my mom from the day I was born. And that's not your fault. It's just ... this is me with all my flaws. If you don't want a divorce, this is what you get. You're dealing with someone who thinks that they aren't worth it."

Cam chuckles mirthlessly. "I don't think I'm worth it, either. I mean, I got left at the altar. Literally." He fingers the papers on the coffee table. "So let me get this straight. You think if we divorce, but I still want to be with you, I'll be proving that I'll stay even if there isn't a legal reason for us to be together."

I nod, then shake my head, then shrug. "Kinda, yeah."

He swallows, and his eyes look sad. "And I'm the opposite. If I sign this, it means I'm accepting that you don't want me."

I inhale sharply. "Oh my god, I didn't think of that."

Cam gulps. "Do you want me?"

"I do. I really do."

"Then don't do this." He squeezes my bicep. "You're not an impossible pain in the ass. You've just been hurt. Let's figure out a way to work through it."

CHAPTER 25

Camden

I head for the shower, shaking with suppressed feelings. Anger. Fear. Mostly dread.

My mind flashes from Leah leaving me at the altar, telling me she didn't love me, to Shelby telling me that we weren't on the same page at all.

I don't want to divorce him, and I don't think he wants to divorce me.

As I wash off the day's sweat and grime, I can't stop thinking about everything that Shelby and I have done together. How far we've come, individually and as a couple—him burning that awful birthday card he'd been carrying like an albatross around his neck, and me letting go of my humiliation and anger over Leah. How much happier I am with him around.

Clearly, I need to talk to someone about this. Once I'm clean and dressed, I make a quick phone call, then pad out into the living room. "Babe, I'm going to go talk with my sister. Do you want me to bring you back anything?"

He shakes his head. I plant a kiss on his forehead, and he sighs. "No."

"Don't move out before I come back," I warn. "We have a lot to talk about. Promise?"

Shelby nods. He looks so forlorn that I just want to gather him up and hold him, but I'm not sure my presence will help. So instead, I get my keys, phone, and wallet, and I drive over to my sister's house in Santa Monica. Charlie calls—she must've called him—and says he's on his way, too.

After she lets me in, she produces a tray of cheese, meats, crackers, and fruit, then pours me a beer and gets herself a glass of prosecco. Charlie arrives ten minutes later and joins us in her living room.

"So why is my big brother here, looking like he's about to burn down Los Angeles?" Reyna asks.

I put my face in my hands. "Shelby has it in his head that when our deal is done—when I'm healed and have health insurance, which is basically now—we need to get a divorce."

"Is that true?" Reyna asks, biting into a slice of apple.

"Well, that's what we agreed at the beginning."

She settles more comfortably on her sectional couch. "That's not what I asked. Is it true that you need to get a divorce?"

I huff. "No. I mean, I don't want to. But he's fixated on an end date. We got married so I could get my ankle taken care of. That's what we agreed."

"And no one ever renegotiates contracts," Charlie says, smearing some brie onto a cracker.

I roll my eyes. "Smartass."

"That's not all that's smart."

Reyna rolls her eyes. "That kind of contribution isn't needed, Charlie." She turns her attention back to me. "I think Shelby likes you, so I wouldn't think he'd want to end things with you."

"Right? But he says he can't believe I'd truly choose him," I say. "I have to figure out how to convince him. That's what I'm here for. Help with that."

Sipping my beer, I stare out her window. It's dark out, now that we're getting close to December.

"So you're asking for us to come up with a grand gesture?" Reyna asks.

"Yeah. I want to show Shelby I love him."

"*Love*?" Charlie asks.

"Yes, *love*. Keep up. I love him."

And, fuck, I do. When I think about living without him, of not having him in my life, it makes my entire body hurt, not just my heart.

"Shelby's the one who's good at that kind of stuff," Charlie says.

"I know," I say, trying not to whine. "I can build things, but I'm sure he could put together a flash mob or order skywriting, or do something else super impressive to get the point across that I love him and want to be with him for the rest of my life."

"Telling him how you feel isn't enough?" Reyna studies my face, then tsks. "You haven't told him you love him, have you?"

"No," I admit. "Okay, I can tell him. But ... I don't know. Should I buy him a better ring? I'm feeling a little guilty about the generic Costco rings. Or should I make him something? Do an Ad/VICE video?"

Charlie coughs. "That worked for Danny, but I'm not sure it's right for you."

"Shelby doesn't seem like the type who needs *things*," Reyna says. "He needs to be loved. Maybe you tell him you're in this for the long haul and ask him to try just one more day with you. Pretty soon those days add up to a life together. I mean, that's what's happened to Mom and Dad." She smiles at me. "Go tell him how you feel."

But this is where I freeze. "How do I know that he still wants me? What if it's like ..."

"Like Leah? Who made you think she was in love with you, but when push came to shove, she didn't want to marry you?"

I nod. In this moment, I feel more vulnerable with my siblings than I ever have in my entire life. I'm the oldest, and I've always been their protector.

I guess now I'm going to find out if they are mine.

"Big brother, you're as bad as Shelby is right now. You're ignoring the evidence right in front of you that Shelby loves you, too. You're not believing that he wants to be with you—"

"He presented me with divorce papers—"

"But he didn't want to. He felt he had to. You're minimizing how he cared for you when you were injured. How his eyes light up when you walk in the room. How I've never seen him as happy as he is when he's with you." She gives me another supportive smile. "You need to take the risk, and he just might surprise you. In any case, there's no other way to find out how he feels."

"At least we know he's not going to ditch you at the altar," Charlie says.

I shoot him a glare. "Thanks for that."

Charlie nods. "Reyna's right. From what I can see, Shelby is in love with you. You're in love with him. So I'm not seeing the big problem."

"I don't know. Don't you think he deserves someone ... better?" I gulp.

"Who better than you? Do you trust anyone else to protect him?" Charlie demands.

"No." Hell no. I'll keep away anyone who tried.

"I think that's your answer." Reyna smiles. "Tell him you love him and you want to be with him."

"That doesn't seem like enough. He was hurt badly by his mom. I'm not sure one person telling him he's loved is going to convince him."

Reyna looks thoughtful. "Then maybe he needs to be reminded of how many people love him besides you." She sits up. "Let me call Noah. I have an idea. We can attack this from multiple angles. We've got you, big bro. We'll help communicate to Shelby that he's worth everything."

"Thank you," I say.

This plan had better work. I don't know what I'll do with my life if I don't have Shelby in it.

* * *

I'm worried what I'll find when I get home—namely that Shelby will have left after all—but he's still there on the couch, playing with his phone, when I walk in.

I don't beat around the bush. "Shelby, I need to tell you how I feel about you." He seems to brace himself for impact, but I keep going. "I don't want to you to leave, but I also don't want to tell you what to do. I'm not going to boss you around."

Because trying to make someone stay when they don't really want to be with you doesn't work. Look at Leah.

"What if I want you to tell me what to do? What if I want you to claim me?" he asks in a small voice. "What if I want you to ask me to stay?"

I get down in front of him on the floor, looking up at him, my hands on his knees. "Then I'm asking you to stay. Shelby, I went over to talk to Charlie and Reyna to try to figure out some big thing I could do to show you that I love you. And we came to the conclusion that the real proof is showing up for you every day. We just have to take a leap of faith that we're both being honest in choosing to do that. Listen to me: *I love you*. I've fallen in love with you, and I want to be with you. And I want to prove it to you every day for the rest of our lives."

His lower lip trembles like a child's, and he looks away. "Fuck. I didn't think it would be this hard."

"What would be this hard?"

"Believing you want me past the expiration date. Believing that you l-l-love me like no one ever has."

My heart beats faster. "I do. I hate that you've gone through so much, because you deserve only good things. But I want you, Shelby. I do. I absolutely love you."

He swallows hard and reaches for me. "I'm sorry I'm so difficult. Can I ask a favor?"

"Anything."

"For now, can you just hold me?"

Settling on the couch, I open my arms. He tucks up into me, and I hold him as long as he wants. I wish I could do more to help him believe me.

CHAPTER 26

Shelby

I don't know the right thing to do.

I want Cam. I'm certain about that part.

He wants me. I think. And he says he loves me. That's astonishing and makes me all confused. So when I wake up in the morning, I do the only thing I can do: get up and go to work.

About two o'clock, after I've been pretty numb all day, someone pauses at the reception desk. I look up and see it's Noah.

"Shelby? Can you come into my office?"

"Am I in trouble?" I don't know why I ask that. I suppose it's a knee-jerk reaction from, oh, my entire life.

He smiles. "Nope. Just a meeting. Demi will cover reception."

"Oh. Okay," I say slowly. I grab a yellow pad and a pen in case I need to take notes.

When we get to Noah's office, I stop. August is sitting in a guest chair. Sam, Alden, and Danny are standing on one side of the office. And there's an extra chair for me in front of the desk.

"What is this?" I ask. "Something about a case?"

"Not this time," Noah says gently.

"It's an intervention," August says.

"But ... I don't need an intervention. I don't abuse any substances."

"That's true," Alden says. "But I think you *were* abused."

The words rake down my back like nails on a chalkboard. All the hairs on my neck stand up. "No."

There's a knock on the door, and Charlie walks in. "Sorry, am I late? Fuck. I'm late." Reyna is right behind him.

"Hi," I say awkwardly, sniffling.

"Cam knows we're here," Reyna says, "but he didn't want to pressure you by being a part of this conversation."

"Right," Noah says. "Besides, we all decided that, as your friends, we needed to talk to you, separate from your husband. Er, boyfriend. Husband?" He shakes his head. "Regardless, you deserve to know how much we all care about you and don't like seeing you hurt. I get that we're not trained professionals in this area. We're not therapists. But lawyers do see a wide swath of the public. And it seems like you might need a little help."

My heart is beating so fast I might pass out. "No," I say, getting up. But Alden stands faster than me.

"You can leave," he says. "But I wish you'd hear us out."

I feel like a trapped animal.

"I think, because someone very close to you hurt you, you're not trusting that someone else won't hurt you now. Let me say that again."

A tear slides down my face. "Evan only did it the one time."

"It's not just Evan," Alden says quietly. "Your entire life, you were betrayed by the person who was most supposed to protect you. Moms aren't perfect, but one who makes you feel like you were a burden? Like you shouldn't have been born?" He shakes his head. "She didn't deserve you. Her opinion of you is not reality. You hear? You're like a fish who can't see the water—the abuse—because you were immersed in it from the moment you were born. But the reality is, you are an amazing human, Shelbs. And you deserve to be loved."

I sniffle. My friends give me kind smiles, and it makes me feel worse. Danny passes me Noah's tissue box, and I take one.

"You dated a bunch of guys who were never going to be right, so you could protect your heart. And then along came Evan," Alden whispers. "The one time you opened your heart. He was supposed to be your boyfriend, your lover, and he betrayed you by lying to you and hitting you."

"We can get you resources if you want to go to a domestic violence survivor group," Noah says gently.

"No," I say, getting frustrated, my hands in fists. "I don't want …"

"You don't have to," Sam says. "But we want you to know that what he did to you is not your fault. At all. The point here is that you had two people close to you who were supposed to protect you, and didn't. That's bound to leave scars."

"Now you've found a great guy," Danny says, "who wants you in the right way."

"Does he love you?" Sam asks.

I nod. "He said he does."

"Yeah. He does. He loves you," Charlie says. "He told us, Reyna and me, but we all see it."

"He told you?" I ask.

Both Reyna and Charlie nod, and something weird happens with my heart. Because it's one thing to tell me, but it's another to tell his family that he's in love.

"The question is, then," Danny says, "do you love him?"

I cough and look around the room. I want to hide, but these people are my best friends. Sure, I work with them, and two of them are literally my bosses. But I know they all care about me on a personal level.

"Too much," I whine. "You guys are too much."

"Answer the question," Alden says gently.

I spin to look at him. "You're the only one in this room besides me who isn't a lawyer, and you're making me feel like I'm on a witness stand?"

"I still note that you're not answering the question," Noah says with a smile.

"Yes. I love him so much," I whisper. "So much that it hurts. So much that the idea of leaving him feels like I'd be leaving a part of myself. But as I say that, I'm having trouble understanding why he wants me."

"Oh, and why is that, Mr. Stubborn?" Charlie asks.

"Because I'm not worth loving," I mutter. I stare at my shoes.

The room is silent.

Noah comes over to me and tugs me to my feet, then gives me a huge hug. He's not Camden, but he's tall and feels comforting. One by one, the rest of my friends wrap their arms around us until we're in this big group hug, and I start laughing. "You guys. You don't have to fix my self-esteem issues."

"Oh, but we do," August says. "Because you having low self-esteem? That's bullshit. You are the *heart* of this office, not just the eyes and ears."

"And what is someone with a heart? Someone who loves and is worth loving," Sam says.

The hug eventually disintegrates, and we go back to our seats.

"We know one group hug isn't going to solve everything," Noah says. "We can help you with therapy or whatever it is you need to heal. But we hope that this is the first stop on the way to you starting to view yourself the way we do. That you are worthy of love, and that we all love you very much."

Alden taps my knee. "What if you were to just act like you were worth something. Same as you acted like things would be okay if you had sex with Cam."

Charlie coughs, and Reyna squeaks. "I like to pretend my brother isn't ... doesn't ... We didn't need to know that," she says.

I raise up my hands. "Sorry. But your brother is smoking hot."

"Anyway," Danny says, taking over. "Alden's right."

Alden smiles. "Thanks."

"Anytime. I know how old programming can take a while to overcome. But I have two more questions for you." Danny leans back in his chair.

"Okay," I say warily. "What are they?"

"Is Camden worth fighting for?"

"Yes," I say immediately.

"And now, the more important question," Danny says, looking around the room. "Are *you* worth fighting for?"

I open my mouth and close it. "I ... um."

"Spoiler alert: the answer is yes," August says, eyeing me significantly.

Chills run up and down my spine. "It's just so uncomfortable to say I'm worth anything."

"You're worth *everything*," Alden says, and all my friends nod.

I bite my lip. "Will you settle for me trying to take your word for it for a while?"

They all look at each other. Sam shrugs. "I think that's fair. What do you guys think?"

"I'm going to lobby for everyone to tell Shelby how much he is loved until he loves himself," August says.

"Aww, babe," Noah says, squeezing his hand.

"You guys are over the top," I say. "You know that? This is too much."

"It's not enough," Alden says.

"And what are you going to do about Cam?" August asks. "Do you still feel like you have to leave him?"

"Or can you let him show you every day how much he loves you?" Reyna asks.

I smile, even though it's a little watery. But I feel like a dam burst. Or something. I know I've been in my own way, and I'm going to try to stop. So I gather my courage and say, "I'm willing to do that."

A low cheer goes up, and it makes me warm inside. "You're going to take it one day at a time with him?" Alden asks.

"Yeah. Yes. Definitely," I say. And saying it makes my heart soar. "Because yes, I do want to stay with Cam. And if I don't have to have everything planned out until the end of time but can just trust that who we are for each other right now is enough—and is growing every day—then that ... that, I can live with."

"Good man," Danny says.

Charlie frowns at a text on his phone. "Also, we need to adjourn this meeting. There's someone I want you to talk to."

I glance at him warily. "Are you going to tell me? Is it Cam?"

"No."

"No to which?" I ask.

Charlie raises an eyebrow. "You'll have to find out."

God, he's frustrating. I sigh loudly and stand. Before heading to the door, I pause and look around the room again. "I love you guys so much. Thank you for doing this."

I get a chorus of "You're welcome" and "We love you" and "You deserve all the best." I need to skedaddle before I start crying again.

As I head toward my desk, Charlie puts a hand at the small of my back, I guess to make sure I don't make a break for it.

"Who is it you want me to talk to?" I grumble. I'm scared it's going to be Cam. I'm scared it's going to be someone else.

I round the corner, everyone trailing behind me, and Camden Cooper, the love of my life, is standing in the reception area, looking distinctly out of place against the building's glossy surfaces. He's facing away from us, wearing a flannel and ripped jeans, and his curls are crushed under a backward baseball cap. His boots are scuffed.

He's never looked better.

Cam turns, and I see he's holding a bouquet of pink roses. And then I notice his smile. At first it's nervous, but it quickly broadens.

"Shelby," he rasps.

I can't help it. I run to him. He holds his arms out, and I slam into his chest so hard he stumbles. "Oh my god, I'm so sorry," I whisper. "Your ankle."

"All healed," he whispers against my cheek. "And sorry I'm not dressed up. I just couldn't wait a minute longer."

And then he's kissing me in front of the whole office. There's a round of applause, but someone, I think Charlie, shushes them. A moment later—too soon—Cam pulls back and hands me the roses.

Then he drops to one knee and holds out a ring box.

CHAPTER 27

Camden

Shelby gasps, the hand that isn't holding the bouquet flying to his mouth.

I feel like I'm putting everything on the line yet again, and I'm hoping that Reyna's plan to gather all Shelby's friends and talk with him has helped. If Shelby will let me, I'm going to tell him every day for the rest of my life how much he matters to me. How much I love him.

Might as well start now.

"Shelby, I'm down on one knee before you, in front of your whole office. And I want to tell you how much you mean to me. I want to share a lifetime of inside jokes, and I want to spend all my days and nights with you."

Someone wolf whistles. I'd wager it's Danny, but I don't know for sure.

"I'd better move this along," I say, "before these guys take over for me. Shelby Borchard, I love you more than I ever imagined I could love someone. I want to spend the rest of my life with you. Would you do me the honor of staying married to me?" My heart is beating so fast I think I might pass out.

The look on Shelby's face makes my stomach drop, and then

he shakes his head. Oh god, I went out on a limb, and he's going to say no.

Fuck. I'm being rejected, in public, in front of a crowd of people I know.

Again.

But then he huffs out a breath. "Camden Cooper, you are unbelievable. Yes, of course. I love you, too."

"So that means you'll stay married to me?" I say hopefully. I hand him a ring that I had engraved with our initials.

"Yes," he whispers, wiping away a tear with the back of his hand. The whole office explodes into applause, and I let out a sigh of relief.

"I don't understand," one of his coworkers whispers, loud enough for me to hear it. "Were they going to split up? I'm so confused."

"I'll explain later," Alden mutters.

I stand and tug Shelby into my arms. "I know this is public as all hell," I say, "and if you want to talk about it more after—"

"No," he says. "I'm certain. But wait a second." He wiggles out of my arms and runs to the back of the reception desk, then returns with something and hands it to me. It's gift-wrapped and feels like a big book.

"What is this?" I ask.

He shrugs. "I made it for you."

While sometimes it feels good to just rip the wrapping off a present, this feels like I need to be a bit more reverent and careful. Not just with the packaging, but with Shelby's heart.

"Open it up," Charlie calls.

"Hush," I say. I slide the tip of my finger under the tape on one side, and it gives easily. Soon I've exposed a photo album. I give Shelby a kiss. "Wow."

"Okay, everyone, let's give them some privacy," Noah calls. People nod and call out their congratulations as they disperse, and soon it's just me and Shelby.

"Did you make me a scrapbook?" I ask.

He bites his lip. "Yeah." His voice sounds scratchy.

I learn why the moment I open the album. The first page is our wedding-day photo, alongside one I didn't know Charlie or, more likely, Alden had taken of us kissing.

My finger traces the edge of the photo. "Damn."

Shelby doesn't say anything, and I turn the page. Our wedding license is next, followed by a shot of us at lunch that afternoon that the server insisted on snapping for us.

I take a seat in one of the reception chairs, and as I go through the album, I see that Shelby has filled it with dozens of memories from the past few months.

Every little slip of paper from a cookie.

A photo of the Ferris wheel at the Santa Monica Pier.

Stills from *Star Wars* showing OSHA violations and HR problems.

The menu from the brunch place we went for his anti-birthday.

An image from the video of us painting the living room, arm in arm and splattered in pale yellow.

A photo from our ski trip, clinking champagne glasses before a fire.

Shelby's documented me falling in love with him.

When I see the time-lapse photos of the different projects we completed to rehab the house and then some sleepy selfies in bed, a tear runs down my cheek.

"Wow." It's hard to speak through the lump in my throat. "I don't know what to say."

"Sorry," he whispers. "I didn't want to overstep—"

"No," I say hastily. "I love it. I absolutely love it, and I love all the care you put into making it. It's the best present I've ever received in my life."

"It's kind of a mess—"

"It's beautiful." He looks so little and forlorn, and I need to figure out how to say this right. "Come here," I demand, and open my arms. He climbs into my lap and snuggles against me. I let him do it for a moment, then pull back so I can see his face. "I love you, do you understand? And the fact that you made something like this is incredible. I want you in my life. In my bed. Every day."

Shelby sniffles. "I wanted to make something to commemorate our marriage, but then I didn't give it to you because I worried it would be manipulative or something."

"Manipulative? To show our love? Not at all." I grin and kiss him.

"And it isn't very fancy. Other people make them look better."

"Stop. Just because it doesn't match something on Pinterest or wherever doesn't mean that it's bad. It means that you made it. And that's the important thing." I sigh. "Look. You and I both like to be creative. You do it with your crafting, and I build houses, but at the end of the day we both value things that have substance."

He nods. "Yeah."

"This book shows that our relationship has substance. It might have started as something that was just for convenience, but it's become pretty damned real."

"It has," he says.

"Do we get to have another ceremony?" I ask.

"If you want one, sure. I think that would be very cool."

God, I love this man. He gives me what I want—and doing so makes him happy.

I know, because I feel the same way about him.

* * *

Noah lets Shelby leave early, and I follow him home in my truck. When we stumble inside, I pick him up and kiss him.

"I'm in love with you," I mumble against his lips.

"I love you, too. In my heart, you're simply mine."

His.

I'm *his*.

I'm *so* his. I want to be his until the end of time.

I can't wait long enough to get to the bedroom, and we end up sprawled out on the living room floor. I don't care about rings or ceremonies or legal documents. All that matters is that the man I love for real loves me back. For real.

Our tongues slide together as we kiss deeply. I grip his waist and flip us over so that he's under me, and Shelby spreads his legs eagerly. I want us to be like this forever. Touching. Caressing. Grinding.

We always had the friendship—even when we barely knew each other, we got along just fine. And I always found him compelling.

But now? It's so much better.

Soon, our makeout session has gotten hot and heavy, and our clothes are shed. Luckily, we've started keeping lube in the coffee table drawer. When I have him prepped, I thrust inside, making us both groan loudly.

"God," he says. "I will *never* get used to that. So good. Never."

"I hope you're *always* used to it," I say. "Because I hope to do it every chance I can."

I do an experimental out-and-in, and when I can tell that he's able to handle it, I start fucking him for real.

"I love how you do this," he whispers. "It's the same as when you hit a nail, with precision and no wasted effort."

That makes me chuckle. "If you're this coherent, I need to do better." I pull out, slap his hip and help turn him over, then enter him from behind.

"I love it this way," Shelby gasps. "I love when you take what you want from me. I love the fact that I can give it to you."

"I will always give you what you need," I promise. I yank him up so he's kneeling and flush with me, which makes my thrusts shallower. Also faster. This is the perfect position to make him blow, since I'm rubbing against his prostate over and over and over again.

I reach around to stroke him, and he orgasms fast but long, the pleasure of it running through him in waves I can see as well as feel.

A few more thrusts—less precise than before—and I'm coming, too, my pulsing dick filling Shelby and making my movements messy and wet.

Then I lean forward, finding his lips, and kiss him deep, not withdrawing until my spent cock slips out of his body. Fluid drips down the inside of my leg, and I love it because it feels like he belongs to me.

And now I know for sure he's mine.

We collapse on the rug, which I know I'll have to clean. But right now, nothing matters other than the two of us.

"You mean it?" I ask.

He knows me so well, he doesn't ask what. "Yeah. I love you. I want to marry you—er, stay married to you. I want to be with you forever. Can we do that?"

"Yes, please."

I kiss him softly as our breathing evens out. "What kind of wedding to you want to have? Something on the beach or in the forest?"

"Hmm. I haven't really thought about what my real wedding would be." Shelby grins. "Actually, I think my fantasy wedding would be eloping with the man I love to the clerk's office."

"Since we did that already, do you want to take some time to plan, so you can do all kinds of wedding crafts? Would that be fun? I'll help," I say.

"And this is why I love you. Because you know me, support me, and want me to have the things that make me happy. Of course I'll marry you. As many times as you want. I'm yours, with no expiration date."

CHAPTER 28

Shelby

On a weekend afternoon in late December, I roll up my pant legs and step with bare feet onto the cool sand. Cam finishes cuffing his suit pants in turn and follows me onto the beach, also barefoot.

"You ready?" he murmurs, clasping my hand.

"So ready."

"Then let's do this."

I grin. "Let's do this *again*." Before we start walking, I pause to gaze at Cam for a moment, processing how lucky I am. The breeze ruffles his hair, and he looks dashing in a dark suit and tie. As for me, I'm wearing the same clothes I wore for our wedding last summer—the flowered shirt and blue suit.

Here I am with this absolute dreamboat, a man who has proved that he would throw himself in harm's way for me, and he's agreeing one more time to be mine forever. I'm the happiest person on the planet.

The soft love reflected in his dark eyes tells me he's *honored* to be with me, that our union is something he wants, too. That he's happy to be with me, perhaps almost as much as I'm happy being with him.

While I'm a work in progress, he's beginning to help me see that I deserve nice things. Like him.

After all, even if my life is messy sometimes, it can still be beautiful.

We're on the secluded beach by Julian Hill's house. Cam's family and our closest friends are standing at the shore in a semicircle, waiting for us. Everyone is full of smiles.

The Pacific Ocean spreads out before us, and the wind has died down, so it's just a cool winter's day on the beach. As we stroll forward, holding hands, I notice how the setting sun turns the water silver.

Most of our friends are in sensible sweaters or pea coats, because even though winter in LA is mild, it's definitely not hot. As we approach the group, I reach up on my tiptoes to speak into Cam's ear. "You look so handsome."

He gives me his widest smile and squeezes my hand. "You stole my line. I love you in that suit." His voice drops. "I love you out of it, too. I love you in anything, honestly." I stop and stare into his eyes, about to pull him to me—

"Hey, no kissing until after the ceremony," Charlie calls, and everyone laughs.

Cam and I grin and walk out to the part of the beach where we're going to have our vow renewal ceremony. We asked Julian Hill to be our MC—seriously, what is my life right now?—and he looks striking in a dark blue velvet tux. Sam, in a bow tie and cardigan, is nothing but heart-eyes for his man. But I only glance at them. The man I care about is right at my side.

Jules welcomes everyone and then says, "Camden Cooper and Shelby Borchard are already married in the eyes of the law as well as in their hearts. But they wanted all of you to be witnesses to how their love has grown and to express their appreciation for the role that each of you plays in their lives." He turns to me. "Shelby, do you want to go first?"

I nod and pull a piece of paper from my pocket. As the sun

sinks into the Pacific, I squeeze my husband's hand, and, surrounded by a group of people who remind me every day that I am loved, I start talking.

"Camden Cooper, I always had a crush on you. From the moment I first saw you, I swear, you were made for me. But I never thought I had a chance with you. When you crashed into my life, almost literally, I knew you were someone special. Anyone who would protect me like that, who would risk getting hurt for me, who would unconditionally support me when I was being wronged? That was someone I wanted. Our marriage may have started out unconventionally, but there's nothing fabricated about the way I love you. I love you so much it's hard to express." I'm surprised not to hear a "How hard is it?" joke out of Charlie, but I see the sparkle in Cam's eye and know he's thinking it. I smile at him, hoping he can see everything I'm feeling. "Will you do me the honor of staying married to me?"

"Absolutely yes," Cam says fervently.

"Cam, would you like to say your vows?" Jules asks.

"Thanks. Yes, I would." Cam clears his throat and makes sure I'm looking at him as he talks without any notes. "Shelby, my vows to you are simple: I vow to love you until death do us part. I vow to take care of you when you need to be taken care of and to listen to you when you need to be listened to. I promise to show up for you every day and to talk through anything we need to talk through, whether it's serious or silly. I love you more than you will ever know."

Cam leans in to kiss me, but there's a tsk from the audience, and he grins at them, then runs a hand through his hair. He clears his throat. "Shelby, I promise to show you every day that I love you, but, more importantly, that you are lovable. I promise to remind you of that and to take care of you. I promise to protect you from harm and to communicate with you. And most of all, I promise to love you for the rest of my life. Would you do me the honor of staying married to me?"

"Yes," I squeak. "So much yes. Can I kiss him now?" I ask Jules, who chuckles.

"I think so," he says warmly. "Let us all congratulate Cam and Shelby on their renewed love."

Cam leans down and kisses me softly. When we break apart, he snakes an arm around my waist and addresses everyone. "Thanks, everyone, for coming. We want to let you all know how much we love and appreciate you as well. To my siblings who show up when I need them with food, transportation, or tough love, whether or not I'm too prideful to ask, and Shelby's coworkers, who give him unconditional support and a sounding board to help him sort things out—we are grateful for your roles in our lives."

I nod. "It's hard to express how much we love you all. Thank you so much."

The applause that surrounds us feels like another group hug.

Cam waves his hands. "Okay, thank you all for coming. Party at Sam and Jules's house. Shelby and I will meet up with you in a few." Then he picks me up in a firefighter's carry and takes off running down the hard wet sand of the beach while I shriek in laughter. Our friends hoot and holler as we leave them in the dust.

"Guess your ankle's better," I gasp.

"Absolutely," he pants.

When we get a ways away from our friends, he shifts me around so I can wrap my legs around his waist, and he ravages my mouth as the cold water laps at his ankles. "I love you so much, you have no idea."

"I have some idea," I whisper. "Because if it's anything close to how I feel for you, it's overwhelming."

"That it is, Shelby. That it is."

When Cam and I finish making out (and, ahem, doing other things), we return to Sam and Jules's home, where everyone is gathered, eating appetizers and drinking champagne.

"There you guys are!" Reyna calls.

"Don't tell us what you were doing," Charlie says, and everyone laughs.

"I'd like to make a toast," Alden says, and we all look at my sweet, awkward best friend, who is getting braver by the day. "To Camden and Shelby. May their love grow and grow."

Everyone raises their glasses. "To Camden and Shelby."

"Kiss!" Danny says, so we do, and everyone cheers.

When the room quiets down a little bit, Jules takes out an acoustic guitar, and we all stop what we're doing. He clears his throat. Given who he is, his smile is surprisingly shy as he starts speaking. "I got to thinking about your love story. You told me and Sam that you eloped, but then when I found out more about it, about how much you two had helped each other and sacrificed for each other, I was inspired to write a song. So, if you don't mind, I'd like to sing it to you as a vow renewal present."

I blink and whisper in my husband's ear, "Um, Cam, do you mind the biggest rock star in the world serenading us?"

"It's amazing," he murmurs back.

"We'd love to hear it," I say.

Jules nods and takes a seat, then strums his guitar. "It's called 'Enough.'"

After playing an intro in a minor chord, he starts singing about how one person escaped a tough family and said, "That's enough." A stranger rescued him from being hurt, saying, "Enough is enough." Their relationship grew, and "Love became enough." The final verse describes how even though they were powerful as one, "Each is enough on their own."

I lose it, tears streaming down my face as I clutch Cam's hand. His face is damp, too. The world seems to shift as Jules puts our story into musical form, and between his soulful voice and the quiet guitar, the song is pure magic.

When Jules finishes, the entire room is sniffling, then bursts into vigorous applause.

"What I wanted to say," Jules says, "is that yes, you two love each other, and you are loved by all of us, but you also *are* love and are *worthy* of love on your own."

"Thanks," I whisper. "That's amazing. And it's not just us, you know? That song is for everyone."

Jules smiles. "Yes, I think it is."

Cam kisses me, and for the rest of the evening, we mingle with our friends and loved ones—who are the same.

* * *

I skip into the bowling alley we rented for our firm holiday party, tugging Cam along with me, both of us laughing.

"Hello!" I call.

"The newlyweds!" Alden replies, and there's a round of applause.

It's not really new, since we've been married for a while now. But we're newly remarried? Newly married for real? Newly married for love?

That's it: we're *love* newlyweds, and I'm enjoying every moment of it.

Cam's face is flushed, because I blew him right before we left to come here, and his hair is a mess from when I kissed him after and mussed it up. Not sorry.

He doesn't look sorry in the least, either. Not when he slings an arm around me and pulls me to him, kissing the top of my head and then leaning down to kiss my lips.

"Get a room!" Charlie yells.

"We already did!" I yell back, and everyone laughs.

I'm so happy. Against all my expectations, I found a man who protects me and treats me the way I want to be treated. One who is kind and generous and giving and better than anyone else I've ever met.

And he's hot, too. Like, damn.

Even though it's awkward with so many people around, I can't seem to let go of his hand—and he doesn't seem to want me to. Both of us have spent enough time on our own, or alone in crowded rooms. Those days are over.

And yeah, I'm happy. I'm allowed to be. I'm adjusting my happiness thermostat to go up and up and up. I've learned that I don't have to always be waiting for the other shoe to drop. Things don't have to go wrong just because they've gone right.

I've started believing in love, in things getting better and better, and in the true heart of the man I married.

When I was scheduling the party, I made sure to order all our favorite foods, so we get plates and join the crowd. Cam still doesn't leave my side. He's not controlling. He just likes to touch me and be affectionate.

I lean into that affection like a purring cat.

"I'm really glad I had that roofing job last summer," Cam murmurs in my ear. "I'm not going to say that breaking my ankle was the best thing to happen to me, but everything that happened after that led me to the love of my life. And to understanding more about myself."

"Both of those things are important," I agree.

"But the most important thing I learned is to keep showing up for you every step of the way."

I smile. "And I'll do the same for you."

"Sounds like we have a new deal," he says, and kisses me again.

Epilogue—Camden

"Ten! Nine! Eight! Seven! Six!"

I tug Shelby to me as our friends and a throng of others loudly count down the seconds to midnight. We're in the middle of the dance floor at One, holding our breath for the clock to change.

"Three! Two! One!"

"Happy New Year!" Shelby and I both shout.

Shelby tilts his head up, and I lean down to kiss him hard. As confetti swirls around us, balloons drop, noisemakers sound, and couples around us kiss.

I'll never get used to how good he tastes or how much I love kissing him.

I hoist him up, and he wraps his legs around my waist. Now that I'm fully healed, this is my favorite way to hold him. I grip him by the ass and ignore all the activity around us, focusing only on making out with my husband. We're still going hot and heavy as we hear other couples around us starting to sing "Auld Lang Syne."

We're both hard and panting, but I'm not stopping, and neither is he. I suppose we should find somewhere more private, but I really don't care. I'm sure worse has been done on this dance floor than a dirty kiss.

When we finally break apart, I mutter in his ear, "I'm so fucking glad it's the New Year and we're still together."

Shelby grins and hugs me even closer. "Yeah, this was going to be our deadline."

"No more. We have no deadline. I want forever with you. I said until death do us part, and I meant it."

"Me, too."

Still carrying him, I make our way through the crowd to an open booth, where I sit down with him straddling me. He drops his lips to my ear, tickling me. "I love you, Camden Cooper."

"I love you, too." I smile at him. "Now what would you like to do?"

He grins. "I think we have the rest of our lives to figure that out. But for now, how about continuing to make out with your husband."

"Sounds like an excellent plan."

* * *

Two weeks later, Shelby's acting like a little kid, and it's adorable. We scan our tickets and go through the turnstiles, heading under the bridge and down to Main Street, USA.

"We're going to have so much fun today!" he gushes. "What do you want to go on first?"

"Pirates of the Caribbean," I say. "You?"

"Adventures in Gardening."

I furrow my brows. "What's that?"

"The boats in Storybook Land. Everyone laughs at me because I like all those little houses and the topiaries, but ..." He shrugs unapologetically, and I love that he feels safe telling me about something other people mock.

"I like that ride, too," I say. "It's outstanding landscaping."

He tugs on my arm. "Wait, we need to stop here first." We walk into the guest center and get pins that say "Just Married," and for the rest of our day at Disneyland, we're congratulated by every cast member we see—and a lot of other people as well. We get the Small World song stuck in our heads and laugh at the bad jokes on the Jungle Cruise, and in short, we have an amazing time.

I hold his hand the entire day. "When we get home, do you want to make some new vision boards?" I ask. "Because I think you're on your way to getting everything on the most recent one."

"Still need a million dollars," he reminds me.

"We'll get money. What else do you want?"

Shelby shrugs and looks around at people in Jedi costumes walking around in what he calls *Star Wars* Land. "Think we can find someone here to talk to about galactic HR practices?"

I laugh. "Sure. And let's go on the *Millennium Falcon* to see how well it banks in space."

"I'll check them for galactic OSHA violations." He smiles, then his expression turns achingly sincere. "I don't know what else I want to put on a vision board. All I know is that I want to spend my future with you."

"Good thing that's what I want, too." We line up for the next ride, happy to be here.

And this is only the beginning. I have a lifetime of showing him how much I love him to look forward to.

* * *

Thank you so much for reading! If you want to help this author out, please leave an honest review somewhere. If you'd like to read a bonus scene where Shelby meets Cam, you can either download it here: https://BookHip.com/KTNRBPD or read it on the bonus section of my website: https://www.lesliemcadamauthor.com/

when-shelby-met-camden. It's password protected, so if you're subscribed to my newsletter, you already have access. Don't have my M/M-only newsletter yet? You can subscribe here: http://eepurl.com/hD9a4r

Acknowledgments

As usual, I have many people to thank for their help with this book. Kristy Lin Billuni and Lex Martin helped with the concept. Ian helped me with the specifics of Cam's injury and the timing of his recovery. My husband provided most of the *Star Wars* comments (as well as those about fortune and/or advice and/or affirmation cookies). Katie gave me the idea for Blackest Friday.

Mary Carr, Megan Dischinger, Rachel Ember, J.E. Birk, Katy Cuthbertson, Phala Theng, and Julia Heudorf all provided insightful comments on beta versions. Alicia Z. Ramos edited it, and Virginia Tesi Carey, Jerica MacMillan, and Katy Cuthbertson proofed it. The cover of Allan (he's a new model) was shot by Cory Stierley and designed by Garrett Leigh. Special shoutout to my Facebook group for voting unanimously—seriously, UNANIMOUSLY—that Cam should have pierced nipples because Allan does. I ended up retconning the story because of that poll result.

Thank you all.

Also by Leslie McAdam

Sarina Bowen's World of True North (m/m)

Undone (audio narrated by Iggy Toma and Tim Paige)

Unmanageable (audio narrated by Jacob Morgan and Teddy Hamilton)

IOU Series (m/m)

Ambiguous (audio narrated by Hamish Long and Kirt Graves)

Studious

Delicious (short story)

Oblivious

Curious

Notorious (coming soon)

With J.E. Birk and Rachel Ember (m/m/m)

ILYBSM

TMI (coming soon)

Faster series (m/m)

Off Track (coming soon)

Contemporary Romance (m/f)

All American Boy Series

Boy on a Train (audio narrated by Desiree Ketchum and James Cavenaugh)

Romantic comedies with Lex Martin

All About the D (audio narrated by Stephen Dexter and Ava Erickson)

Surprise, Baby! (audio narrated by Jacob Morgan and Muffy Newton)

The Giving You ... series

The Sun and the Moon (audio narrated by Tor Thom and Charley Ongel)

The Stars in the Sky

All the Waters of the Earth

The Ground Beneath Our Feet (audio narrated by Tor Thom and Charley Ongel)

Love in Translation series

Sol

Sombra

Standalone novella

Lumbersexual (audio narrated by Tor Thom and Charley Ongel)

About the Author

Leslie McAdam is a California girl who loves romance and well-defined abs. She lives in a drafty old farmhouse on a small orange tree farm in Southern California with her husband and two children. Leslie's first published book, *The Sun and the Moon*, won a 2015 Watty, which is the world's largest online writing competition. She's gone on to receive additional literary awards and has been featured in multiple publications, including Cosmopolitan.com. Her books have been Top 100 Bestsellers on both Amazon and Apple Books. Leslie is employed by day but spends her nights writing about the men of your fantasies.

Website: https://www.lesliemcadamauthor.com

M/M-only newsletter: http://eepurl.com/hD9a4r